To Shirle
With best wishes always.
Judy

DOUBLE

JEOPARDY

A NOVEL

JUDITH BLEVINS

Copyright © 2012 by Judith Blevins

Double Jeopardy
By

Judith Blevins

Copyright © 2012 by Judith Blevins

Published by BRASS FROG BOOKWORKS
Grand Junction, CO
www.BrassFrogBookworks.com

Inquiries should be addressed to:

Judith Blevins
2485 Fountainhead Blvd. Unit G 8
Grand Junction, CO 81505-8662

Library of Congress Control Number: 2012931535

ISBN 978-0-9847096-0-1

Printed in the United States of America

March 2012

Cover Design: J L Leon www.ClickCreativeMedia.com

DEDICATION

This novel is dedicated to those who have accompanied me on my life's journey and, despite the many challenges, never left my side.

ACKNOWLEDGMENTS

To all those who encouraged and inspired me to write this novel I am most grateful. Special thanks to my daughter, Shelly Blevins-Lambert, my treasured friend, Pamela Cotharn and to my favorite mystery and legal fiction writer, Carroll Multz. Carroll's sage advice and editing skills contributed greatly to making this novel what it is.

I am the master of my fate; I am the captain of my soul.

Invictus – William Henley

TABLE OF CONTENTS

PROLOGUE

The office was barely adequate to accommodate his small staff consisting of one assistant, Jordan Slater, and her boyfriend, Dave Jennings. The crew from the national weekly television program, *Sincerely Yours,* nonetheless crowded in with their gear leaving little room for much else. Not wanting to miss "the big show" Jordan and Dave scrunched up against the wall where they could watch through the floor-to-ceiling glass panel separating the boss' office from the reception area.

Samuel "Salty" Morton was being groomed by the makeup crew as Linda Bishop, star reporter for *Sincerely Yours*, positioned him behind his massive oak desk while continuously barking orders at her staff and simultaneously giving Salty instructions on how the interview would be conducted. Meanwhile the sound team got him wired with a mic and the cameramen got into position and set up their shot angles.

The nickname, "Salty," initially came from his career as a Navy JAG officer. With the last name of Morton and because sailors were known as "Salts," it just seemed to fit. When he left the Navy and went into the private practice of law the moniker stuck; it didn't take long for him to be equated with the elements of salt. He was known in the legal arena for his ability to not make much ado about nothing and to *take things with a grain of salt*. His level-headedness made *salt of the earth* an appropriate description. He certainly *earned his salt* as his dedication to his clients was universally renowned. He was also touted to *be worth his salt* and, of course, he was theatrical enough to *add flavor* to any court hearing.

Not to be outdone, Mother Nature had lent a hand as well when she determined he should become prematurely gray. Thus when he was 26 years of age his hair started gradually turning and now in his mid-sixties was completely white. The thick unruly mass perched atop his head gave way to vivid blue eyes that never disclosed what he was thinking but could delve deep into another's and determine what was hidden beyond. He could have made a fortune playing poker. Morton, although mature, was still handsome in that "Clark Gable" way, mustache and all. He sported broad shoulders. His athletic build was enhanced by his inviting smile and hypnotic voice. He was Navy tough and military rigid. His demeanor transmitted the message he was not to be toyed with and not many challenged him physically. Those who did regretted it. His integrity was irreproachable and he was highly respected by prosecutors, defense attorneys and judicial personnel alike.

Suddenly and without warning, bright lights flooded the office. Salty blinked. The television crew began filming and Bishop launched into the introduction of the *Sincerely Yours* interview in her practiced "on air" voice.

"I'm here in Farmington, New Mexico," she began, gazing into the camera, "with this year's winner of the prestigious defense bar's *Lifetime Achievement Award.* A panel, consisting of a variety of legal experts including judges, prosecutors and defense attorneys along with legislators and state senators, review candidates and make the selection. To even be considered for this award is an honor in itself. The *Lifetime Achievement* panel selected Attorney Samuel Morton to receive this year's honor due to his brilliant career in the defense of the innocent who may have otherwise been convicted of crimes they had not committed."

"Mr. Morton, better known among his collogues as "Salty" has agreed to be interviewed by *Sincerely Yours*. Sir, may I call you Salty?"

"Of course. I'm rarely referred to by any other name and may not recognize to whom you are speaking if you continue to call me Mr. Morton and drop the 'Sir,' I left that behind when I left the Navy."

"Okay, Salty it is," Bishop continued. "Over the span of forty years you have undoubtedly dealt with many clients and situations too numerous to list. With this in mind, we previously asked you to select one special case, a case that stands out in your memory that you would like to focus on in this interview. We, of course, would like to delve deeply into the archives of your exciting career but time constraints prohibit us from doing so." Bishop turned and smiled into the camera. "I'm now going to turn the interview over to Salty and let him tell us, in his own words, about his most fascinating career case."

He had selected the first degree murder case of *People of the State of New Mexico v. Jasmine Zachary*. In preparing for this interview, he had relived the events that led up to the most notorious trial in San Juan County's history. Because of his near photographic memory, even tiny details loomed large in his mind as he remembered Jas. The camera now focused on Salty, then pulled back slightly. His hands rested lightly on the desk in front of him. He pressed his lips together for a moment and exhaled slowly as the memories of the case took shape in his mind.

PART ONE

…and so it begins…

CHAPTER 1

CLEAR AND SUNNY

The end of July in Farmington, New Mexico, lived up to its predictable promise of being hot – miserably hot in fact. Saturday's five o'clock evening Mass at Holy Trinity Catholic Church was not as crowded as usual because many church-goers were vacationing or planning to attend the much cooler Sunday morning Masses. Because Jas worked five days a week, she seldom deviated from her routine to "get church out of the way" Saturday evening. She could then lounge around Sunday mornings not having to meet a time schedule. Living alone and having been

2

widowed several years before, she usually breezed through Sundays just enjoying her time off.

As the July heat pressed in upon the congregation, the Mass droned on and on with the redundant sermon and Jas began looking around for consolation from her fellow worshipers. She glanced across the aisle and was surprised to recognize a familiar face from the past – could it be? She stared at the man across the aisle from her as he knelt. Her mind began conjuring up images from forty years before when she was a freshman at Farmington High School and he was a sophomore. She remembered having a severe school-girl crush on him at that time. The priest was chanting: "Glory be to the Father, the Son and the Holy Spirit" and Jas was jerked back into the present when the man in her sight, exhibiting discomfort, gestured toward himself indicating "are you staring at me?" Embarrassed, she looked away. *Good grief, what must he be thinking?* She then wondered if he recognized her as well, *if* it even was him. When Mass ended she hurried out the door hoping not to embarrass herself any further. Still, she couldn't stop wondering if the man across the aisle was Nick McGregor.

For the next few weeks when she attended Mass, the man with the familiar face was also there. Not wanting to attract unwanted attention to herself, she tried to ignore him because she still wasn't really sure it was Nick McGregor. After all, forty years can change one's appearance. However, she couldn't keep from stealing glances every so often. Then on the last Saturday in July, she exited the church after Mass and saw the person she believed to be Nick McGregor standing on the church steps chatting with another parishioner. As she passed the two, a pleasant male voice called out to her.

"Say, aren't you Jasmine O'Connor?

She stopped in her tracks and turned around to see a friendly smile gracing her mysterious stranger's handsome face.

"You look so familiar. Didn't we go to the same high school?"

A twinge of excitement rippled through the pit of her stomach as she returned his smile and extended her hand. It *was* Nick McGregor.

4

"Why yes. I thought I recognized you as well. It's been a long time but you don't seem to have changed much."

He chuckled pleasantly at the compliment. "I'm flattered that you think so, but my mirror tells me otherwise."

"Well then, you need a new mirror," Jas assured him. He threw up his hands in mock surrender, "I don't like to tempt fate. Remember what happened to Snow White when the wicked stepmother's mirror turned on her?"

"Okay then, your lesson for today is to just avoid apples," she joked.

"Excellent advice!" He hesitated a moment as he held her in his gaze. "It suddenly occurs to me that my education in fairytales is somewhat lacking. Perhaps I could persuade you to join me for dinner so you can enlighten me on how to dodge poison apples and other pitfalls." He flashed his captivating smile once again. "Besides, I'd love to get to know you better and catch up with what's been going on in your life."

That was the quintessential heart-stopping moment. Was he serious? Of course she would have

5

dinner with him and, without hesitation, graciously accepted.

They left her car in the church parking lot. Nick escorted her to a polished late model white diamond Cadillac Escalade sitting off by itself. He opened the passenger door and she slid onto the soft, comfortable leather seat and then watched as he climbed in behind the wheel. They drove to the River Side Restaurant, known for its charming elegance and fine food. Once inside the restaurant and having ordered dinner, the conversation became lively and surprisingly comfortable as they brought each other up to speed on the last forty years. It felt like they had always known each other.

Nick told Jas, that upon graduation from high school he did a stint in the Air Force where he learned to fly. He discovered flying was in his blood and he became addicted to it. When he left the Air Force, he went to work for World Wide Airlines as a captain and flew internationally for the next twenty-five years. Nick said he had married but his wife, Stephanie, had died a few years before from ovarian cancer.

Nick then became quiet and reflective. What he did not tell Jas was that after Stephanie died, he became depressed and secluded himself even to the extent of not going to church. He didn't want to be around people. He was harboring guilty feelings. The death of his wife didn't cause his depression; his guilt at having not loved her did. When he came to grips with the guilt he began going back to church and prayed that God and Stephanie would forgive him for his lack of love for her and the charade their marriage turned into.

Jas shifted in her chair as she watched Nick and waited for him to continue. Nick, suddenly realizing he was distracted said, "I have four daughters and am blessed with seven grandchildren. My daughter, Nicole and her husband Jason, or Jay as we call him, live locally with three of my grandchildren. Molly is twelve, Tony is ten and Suzy is eight. My swimming pool may be one reason I get to see them regularly in the summer, otherwise its catch-as-catch can. My other daughters are all married and scattered across the country. We do try to get together and have a yearly family reunion but there is usually one or two who can't make it. I remember how difficult it was to go places when the kids were in school. Even the summers were filled with running here-and-there participating in sports and other summer activities. Since I've retired, I take time to do the things I like so sometimes I rent a puddle-jumper and go see them. I should take you up into the wild blue yonder someday and give you the bird's eye view of how enchanting the desert is from the air."

"It sounds wonderful!" exclaimed Jas. "I'd *love* it."

He took a sip of his wine and smiled. "You will then understand why New Mexico is called *The Land of Enchantment.* Flying over the Grand Canyon is truly a treat. You have no idea of the vastness until you've seen the Colorado River from above. God must have been in seventh heaven, literally, when He created the Grand Canyon. Say, if you're not in a hurry, after we finish here maybe you would like to drop by my house and see the giant catfish I've been cultivating in a pond on the 'south forty.'"

Another heart-stopping moment. Was he serious? Of course, she would like to come by and instantly told him so.

After a pleasant dinner, they climbed back into Nick's car and, with the open sunroof exposing the beautiful desert evening sky, drove to the McGregor estate. The massive Spanish-style structure perched on top of the hill was somewhat of a local landmark. The property was surrounded by intricate wrought iron fencing and high stucco walls that matched the color of the surrounding desert. Jas remembered admiring it from her high school days. Nick nosed the car up the hill along a road that cut through the center of the property. All along the road and fringing the front of the house, was an explosion of color and gently swaying Pampas grass on the meticulously landscaped grounds. The road opened into a sweeping cobbled drive that widened into a plaza in front of the house. In the center of the plaza was a huge stone fountain with water cascading into a pool at its base and surrounded by colorful plantings. Nick stopped in front of the house and killed the engine. When he opened the door for Jas, she stepped out and stopped for a moment, pivoting her

9

head back and forth as she tried to take it all in. Zanadu was the first descriptive adjective that popped into Jas's mind. She had often wondered what it would be like to live there and never *dreamed* that she would ever have the chance to go inside.

"Nick, this is more beautiful than I ever imagined!"

He smiled and took her arm, leading her onto a massive veranda that ran the full width of the house, and through a set of huge hand-carved doors. She was greeted by an immense entryway artfully set with colorful tiles and a high vaulted ceiling. The pleasant coolness of air conditioning felt good as she followed Nick through a wide archway flanked by thick columns and into a comfortable living area. The entire back wall of the room was glass revealing a tennis court with a shaded seating area, and a spectacular pool off to the right.

"If you'd like the 'twenty-five-cent tour' you can put your things over there." He stabbed his finger toward a large couch that hugged the curve of the wall.

"I'd love it!" she exclaimed.

Nick led her from room to room. The six bedroom four bath home was tastefully decorated in a Spanish-style theme to match the architecture. Even though some of the décor was dated, each room they visited was even lovelier than the last. Jas was sure that the kitchen was larger than her entire condominium. The warm rich wood of the cabinetry, the state-of-the-art appliances, and a huge expanse of polished marble counter tops took her breath away. A wide window spanned the entire length of the room and looked out over the desert, making the kitchen feel even larger. They finished the "tour" with a stop in the media room, then into a comfortable library with a large fireplace, massive overstuffed furniture and some impressive bronze sculptures. Finally they settled in on the patio in a large canopied swing adjacent to the pool.

"This is fantastic!" Jas exclaimed. "It's like having a city park all to yourself. If I lived here I would think I had died and gone to heaven."

"It is all that," Nick responded. "However, it does have its drawbacks. I just recently lost my live-in maid due to college graduation. She decided to find a real job and apply her degree. I'm having trouble

11

finding a replacement. Those who have applied are either too old or too young or don't possess the desired qualifications."

"I think I know what you're referring to. Unless they're a ten, you don't want them."

"What? Are you clairvoyant on top of everything else? Looks as though I better be careful not only in what I say but what I think." Both laughed as each stared into the eyes of the other.

After a long moment, Jas said, "Our faith teaches us that you can sin in what you think as well as in what you do. Those thoughts about the coveted maid didn't escape me or the Lord."

Looking heavenward, Nick said, "*Mea culpa, mea culpa, mea maxima culpa.*"

Jas just shook her head in contrived disgust and said, "You better say a perfect Act of Contrition to be forgiven for your sinfulness."

"I don't think salvation is in the cards. My paradise, as you earlier described it, is here and now." For an awkward moment Nick looked down and bit his lip. Jas realized it was time to change the subject.

"When did you return to Farmington?" she asked brightly, changing the course of the conversation.

"I moved my family back here shortly after the deaths of my parents. It will be twenty-two years ago this coming January. You no doubt read about my parents being killed in a traffic accident on their way home from a New Year's Eve celebration at the country club."

"I read about that. What a terrible thing. I think the newspaper said they were the victims of a hit-and-run accident and it was never determined who was responsible."

"Some days later they interviewed a local drunk who they suspected was involved. However, he cleverly claimed his damaged pickup was stolen. Since it was recovered on the outskirts of town and the drunk's brother vouched for his whereabouts, no arrest was ever made."

"So without any brothers or sisters, you inherited this estate. Do you miss Albuquerque?"

"Not really. I always loved Farmington and the home place. After moving back, for years I commuted to Albuquerque, my home base. Since I flew internationally, I only worked ten days a month. That equated to two round trips per month from Farmington to Albuquerque. The commute was never much of a hassle."

"Having lost my own parents in a boating accident at Lake Powell, I know how devastating it is to lose both parents at the same time. When I read about your parents, I tried to get in touch with you to express my sympathy. Unfortunately, I was unable to obtain your address."

Nick gently squeezed Jas' arm in a gesture of his own sympathy. "I never really kept in touch with anyone after high school. This is the first I've learned of your parents' tragic deaths. I'm so sorry."

Both sat in silent reflection. Finally Nick said, "You haven't told me much about what you've been doing these past years. I remember you from high school. You cut quite the cute figure in your cheerleading outfit. Purple and white, fight, fight, fight!" He threw back his head and laughed. "If I hadn't been going steady with 'Sandra Dee,'" he teased, "I certainly would have dated you even though you were a 'freshman puke.'"

"Ha!" Jas laughed and rolled her eyes at him. "I'm not so sure. You were the 'big man' on campus and very popular. Plus, as you just so eloquently pointed out, I was just a freshman puke," she sneered.

"Now, now, don't be bitter. Sandra, of course, thought she was the cat's meow! I suspect having wealth in the family increases one's opinion of one's self. You should've seen her when you were voted Homecoming Queen. She was livid."

Jas smiled to herself as she conjured up an image of her moment of glory and of Sandra being livid. *Served her right,* Jas mused.

Nick continued the stroll down memory lane: "One of the fondest memories of my high school years was the time you and I were alone in the school library and you boldly walked up to me and kissed me sweetly on the lips. I still think about that and how that affected me emotionally. It was so unexpected. You were always the shy type. You really threw me for a loop. I almost went into shock. Guess you thought big, bad football heroes were immune to shock?" He raised his eyebrows and smiled. "So, bring me up to speed.

What's happened in your life since high school? I've been doing all the talking."

"Well, I admit you were rather dashing in your football uniform and I had a super crush on you. But, I suspect you knew that and if you didn't, you were dead from the neck up. As for the kiss, I've been known to be impulsive and spontaneous and that was one of those rare moments. Now that I think about it, you responded to the kiss. You amazingly recovered rather quickly from the 'shock.'" Jas pursed her lips and rubbed her chin lightly. "You still think about that? Interesting! I'd completely forgotten until you mentioned it."

"Liar!" Nick humorously quipped. "And, of course I responded. That has to be every seventeen-year-old boy's second favorite dream."

"I'll not ask what the first is," said Jas. Nick smiled at her and Jas blushed. So much for playing it cool.

"Okay, you win! I must admit, it's true. I do think about it and you occasionally." *If only you knew,* Jas thought.

Continuing, she said, "I own my own business, *Interior Designs by Jasmine.* Zack, my husband, died

16

five years ago of a heart attack while hunting. He was much too far from civilization to get medical help and the autopsy revealed that it would have been futile anyway. His years of smoking contributed to the deterioration of his health and the exertion of hunting that day was the catalyst that finally killed him. After Zack died, I took some classes in interior design as I've always had a desire to do so and discovered I had a knack. I opened my own shop and have been fairly successful. We didn't have children. Not that we didn't want to. It just didn't happen. We talked about adopting but eventually decided against it."

Nick quietly said, "It's now my turn to convey sympathy. I'm sorry to hear of your loss. I, of course, didn't know as I was pretty much out of touch with the local happenings after moving to Albuquerque." Then, after a pause, attempting to get the conversation back on a lighter note, he asked "Jasmine is an unusual name. Is it a family name?"

"Oh no, but it just didn't come out of the blue. Sometimes don't you just have to wonder how people come up with names? My mother's favorite flower was the gardenia, however, my father strenuously objected to naming me 'Gardenia,' for which I am eternally grateful. After much 'discussion' they agreed on 'Jasmine' since the flower is a smaller version of the gardenia and the fragrance almost identical. Not too exciting, but that's how it happened or so I've been told all my life. And you?"

"That's quite a story and bless your father for his insight. I like the name 'Jasmine,' but may I call you 'Jas'? Just between friends. It's less formal."

"Yes, please do, everyone does and I much prefer it." Jas responded.

"My story is not quite as interesting but a bit more logical. Would you believe I was born on Christmas Eve? However, I seriously doubt my parents named me after *Jolly Ole Saint Nick*. My complete name is Nicholas Matthew McGregor. My folks aspired to having four sons and naming us after the four apostles, Matthew, Mark, Luke and John. That's why my middle name is 'Matthew.'" They only had me. I often wondered how different my life would have been if I'd had three younger brothers. However, I'm sure when I reached my teen-years my parents were grateful

18

they only had one." After a short pause, Nick asked, "Are you presently seeing anyone?"

A soft breeze helped ease the awkwardness surrounding the unexpected question.

Jas answered: "No, not at all. Since Zach died, I've been what you call a 'born-again virgin.'"

"Born-again virgin, that's cute, I like that. I didn't ask you if you were...."

"I know. Knee-jerk reaction. Pleading innocent and all that. It's a defense mechanism I've developed the last several years."

"Yep, that ole Catholic guilt rears its ugly head. There's no escaping it once you've been indoctrinated."

"Some things are innate and harder to discard than others. It's the concern about the 'fires of hell' that keep me on the straight and narrow."

Nick was attracted to Jas and wanted to get to know her better. She was so different from the other women he knew and he was fascinated with her. She caught him staring so he said, "Hey, it's getting late. Let me drive you to your car. Where do you live anyway?"

"Actually, not too far from here but compared to this area, it's the slums."

"You're too kind and I don't believe a word of it. I'm not much of a cook but I can put a tolerable sandwich together. Will you come back tomorrow for lunch, say around noonish? Bring your swimsuit and we'll cool off in the pool before we eat. What do you think?"

"How can I refuse an offer like that? Besides, you haven't shown me the giant catfish yet."

"Hopefully, you have a better reason for a return engagement. Believe me, I don't throw bologna and bread together for just anyone. Add a few chips and you got yourself a gourmet meal. You may be surprised at my culinary skills. Hell, even I may be surprised at my culinary skills."

Nick reached over and took her hand and led her up the driveway. He drove her back to the church parking lot. He held the door for her as she got into her car, then stood and watched as she drove away. Jas threw Nick a kiss as she slowly drove past. That little gesture would become a time honored tradition throughout the remainder of their relationship.

CHAPTER 2

SLIGHTLY BREEZY

Rogers and Hart nailed it when they wrote *Bewitched, Bothered and Bewildered* in 1940. The lyrics could not have been more appropriate as to what she was feeling at this moment. "I'm wild again, beguiled again, a simpering, whimpering child again, bewitched, bothered and bewildered am I…" That is exactly how Jas was feeling when Nick invited her over for a day of swimming and relaxation. She felt like an excited schoolgirl, amazed at how comfortable she felt with Nick.

Sunday loomed hot but the pool was cool and the water was dazzling reflecting the sun's rays and intensifying the blue of Jas' bright sparkling eyes. She wore a modest one-piece aqua-colored bathing suit which did justice to her five foot six, one hundred thirty-five pound athletic frame. With her medium length auburn hair pulled up in a banana clip she looked stunning.

Nick looked at Jas appreciatively. He also selected a modest suit foregoing the Speedo he usually wore in order to get as much of his torso exposed to the sun as possible without, of course, transgressing into the realm of indecency.

They had a wonderful time splashing around and engaging in an endless flow of conversation. After about an hour of swimming, Nick got out and smoothed back his hair.

"I don't know about you, but I am starved. Let's see what I can find."

He excused himself and went inside, leaving Jas to soak up the sun. She wrapped herself in a bright colored beach towel and sat on the edge of the pool dangling her feet in the water. A short time later Nick returned.

"Lunch is served," he announced as he came out the sliding glass doors balancing a large tray on one upturned hand. Jas put on her flip-flops and sauntered in Nick's direction as he arranged the tray on one of patio tables situated out of the sun.

"Come sit down," he said, motioning to a comfortable looking chair.

"My, my" she exclaimed as she sat down and surveyed the assortment of meats, cheeses, crackers, fruits and vegetables artfully arranged on a bright colored platter. "Bologna sandwiches indeed. Don't tell me you did this all by yourself!"

"Of course I did. Just ignore the label from Abe's Deli; they try to take credit for all my creations."

They both laughed and began to eat. It was a perfect day. Jas looked into Nick's piercing blue eyes. He was barely balding and he wore his sun bleached hair in a stylish cut. *He is quite distinguished*, she thought as she sized him up. His six-foot, hundred and ninety pound frame was solid for his age. He sported a fabulous tan and was the picture of health.

"Since you've retired, what else do you do to keep busy?" Jas asked as the pair lounged on deck chairs by the pool digesting a surprisingly tasty lunch.

"Oh, this place keeps me hopping, especially since my live-in maid quit. I've been doing it all. I'm the chief cook and bottle washer, housekeeper and pool boy. However, I do have a yard service. They come once weekly and do a good job keeping the place looking respectable. I personally take care of the pool. I like playing in and around the water. And, what do you *mean* by what else do I do to keep busy?" He feigned a stern look. "I don't pick up strange women every day, if that's what you think. But I would if I could." Laughingly he added, "Just kidding, I actually lead a pretty quiet life. Getting excited about football is about the extent of my emotional exertion."

Jas sipped her iced tea and smiled.

"Say," he began, "I got to thinking after you came here yesterday evening that this monstrosity of a house needs some updating. Even though there have been a few things done here and there, it is still the way my mom furnished and decorated it when I was just a kid. That's been longer ago than I care to remember even if I could. How 'bout I hire you to do some cosmetic surgery on this place? Would you be interested?"

Jas almost choked on her tea but tried to sound nonchalant. "I would enjoy working with you on such a project, but it looks beautiful just the way it is. Are you sure you want to trifle with it?"

"Yes, I'm sure. Stephanie wasn't much of a home-body. She didn't have any desire to redecorate and make the place 'hers.' She was more outdoorsy and spent almost all of her spare time outside doing something-or-other. She did, however, have a green thumb. Most of the landscaping I attribute to her talents. Plus she was a superb cook. I had to cut way back to get down to my fighting weight after she died. I also think I compensated for my loss with food for about six-months adding to the tonnage I accumulated while we were married. I am still paranoid and watch my intake pretty closely most of the time. Once-in-awhile I succumb to the lure of ice cream. Man does not live by carrot sticks alone you know. So, my dear, to answer your question, I'm ready for a change." He shrugged slightly. "This place feels like a mausoleum after losing my parents and then Stephanie. There are too many ghosts roaming around. I trust your judgment and expertise and know you will chase them away. What do you say?"

He wants me to redecorate his home! Is this really happening? Guise or no guise, I'm flattered.

"If you like, we could arrange special accommodations for my contract so as not to take you out of your shop for any appreciable length of time. I'm not opposed to evenings and weekends if that would work better for you. I would like to help with the painting, carpenter work and the more 'manly' chores if you agree?" Nick said.

"Sounds like a deal. Evenings and weekends would work best for me. Do you have any idea of what you want and how much you want to spend?"

"Not a clue. When we moved here from Albuquerque, I was able to convince Steph that the kitchen needed an update. She agreed. So, you wouldn't need to do anything much with the kitchen – that is, unless you think otherwise.

"Oh, I agree with you on the kitchen. The cabinets and counter tops are state of the art. I wouldn't change a thing if it were me."

"I haven't thought about it. The inspiration to redecorate just occurred to me while sitting here with you. I don't want to lose the Spanish theme, but I do want to modernize the interior and get rid of the relics.

"We should do a walk-through and perhaps I can make some suggestions. Is that a comfortable place to start?" she queried.

"Up to you. How soon can you begin?"

"We could do a walk-through right now," suggested Jas.

"Today is far too nice to think about work. I was thinking we could relax the rest of the day and then meet tomorrow evening after you close your shop. Would that be convenient?"

"It sounds wonderful. I can keep my shop open during the day and meet here after hours. That would work just fine for me."

Nick smiled and stuck out his hand. "It's a deal."

"Deal!" replied Jas, giving his hand a hearty shake.

"Good. C'mon. Let's go inside and watch the news on Channel 11."

Once inside Nick ushered Jas to one of the guest bathrooms so she could shower and get dressed. He performed a like ritual in the master suite for himself, after which he built each of them a tall glass of his patented ice tea and, with drinks in hand, led her to the den. They situated themselves on an oversized sofa and turned on the television.

Nick moved closer to Jas and, taking her hand in his, said: "Have you thought about intimacy with anyone since your husband died?"

Jas fidgeted nervously for a moment not knowing exactly how to sidestep the question. Finally she looked at him and smiled. "Of course I've thought about it. I may be old, but I'm not dead! I miss the loving a lot but not enough to compromise my religious convictions." To Nick, however, her eyes said otherwise.

He then slid his arm around her waist and pulled her close. She resisted little as Nick gently elevated her chin and kissed her on the lips – tenderly at first and then passionately. His lips were warm and moist and she found herself responding in return. Jas was instantly consumed in a fiery desire that ignited her

28

whole being. She had not felt such desire as this for a long, long time – and maybe never – at least not quite like this.

Jas' heart skipped more than a few beats and she found it difficult to breath for a moment or two as she thought, *He wants me and I want him, but…*

She closed her eyes and before long she gave herself totally and completely to him. The afternoon slipped into evening as they lay in each other's arms, barely talking, just savoring the afterglow. An old grandfather clock somewhere in the house chimed six times before the couple stirred and came to life. When they were dressed, Nick said he would fix a light dinner and Jas, not wanting the euphoric day to end, readily accepted. Once again they sat on the patio and enjoyed the cool evening breeze as she was introduced to his modified version of the western omelet.

"You really can cook, I'm impressed."

"Oh, don't be so impressed. How much talent does it take to throw a couple of eggs together with green chili, ham and cheese?"

"You haven't seen me in the kitchen."

They both endeavored to keep the conversation light not wanting to "spoil" the effect the love-making had on them by saying the wrong thing. Eventually, Nick asked: "Will you come by tomorrow after work?"

Jas tempered the desire to say "YES! YES! YES!" and instead answered: "Sure, I'd love to. Let me help with the dishes. Then I should go."

"I'll get the dishes later. Come on, I'll walk you to your car."

He held the door for her and she blew him a now familiar kiss as she drove off. He waved goodbye.

Jas, alone with her thoughts in the quiet of the night, found she was terribly conflicted between the man she *knew* she deeply loved and a lifetime of religious upbringing. She had succumbed to *the world, the flesh and the devil*, as it were. She didn't want to jeopardize her immortal soul but yet she had to admit she was hopelessly, helplessly and totally immersed in the new-found sensations of being in love and resistance and abstinence were no longer viable options. Would she ever be forgiven? That was something that needed to be pondered – but not this night.

Monday morning pounced like a cat and Jas, having slept fitfully, groaned as she shut off the alarm squawking at her from the night stand. Thoughts of the weekend permeated her consciousness and soon she was consumed with a wealth of new-found energy. She actually leapt out of bed, showered, dressed and left for her boutique. Jas found herself constantly looking at her watch as she interacted with customers and carried out the usual functions of her trade. The day was dragging on even though she was busily occupied. She could scarcely wait for five o'clock to arrive and caught herself smiling as she remembered bits-and-pieces of the weekend; bits-and-pieces, hell, every detail. Finally, the little hand moved to five and the big hand moved to twelve! She went through her closing routine and locked up. She resisted the urge to exceed the speed limit to get home. Once there and while changing into more casual attire, the telephone rang. She answered it on the first ring.

"Hello."

"Hello yourself," Nick said.

"What are you doing?"

"Waiting for you."

"Five minutes?"

"You must be really special as I'm attempting to cook again. This cooking isn't as easy as the Iron Chefs lead one to believe. I've been tossing food and adding a pinch of this and a pinch of that to create what is turning out to be a complete disaster. I'm ready to throw in the towel!"

"I would help you but I'm just as inept in the kitchen as you are," Jas said.

"But not in other rooms I might add..."

"No comment. See you in a few."

Nick met her at the door and gave her a quick hug. "I actually missed you" he said with a smile and a slight blush.

"Likewise. I missed you as well."

"Did you think of me today?" asked Nick.

"Only a few hundred times." Jas replied. "I relived the weekend and how much fun it was."

"Well, that's not very specific." Nick responded.

"I'll have to know you better before I reveal everything including my most intimate thoughts." Jas blushed.

"Well, don't just stand there. Come on in and let me introduce you to a new creation. I call it La Gourmet Ala Frozen Dinner. I gave up on Pheasant Under Glass with a side of Humming Bird Wings."

"You're too funny. La Gourmet sounds like a fine dinner; humming bird wings tickle." They ate dinner on the patio enjoying the evening as the sun vanished over the New Mexico horizon, but not their dreams.

CHAPTER 3

WHIRLWINDS

J as and Nick were soon spending virtually all their spare time together. Little revolved around redecorating the mansion. The days melted into weeks and the weeks into months. Their passion for each other was almost insatiable. They became more relaxed with each other and, having grown up in the same era, found that they had many and varied things in common. The two of them enjoyed the same kind of literature, music, food and fun. They spent quiet evenings reading to each other or watching television. Their senses of humor "jelled" and they found themselves laughing a lot over anything and everything.

By this time, Jas was completely entrenched in the relationship. She often told Nick how much she loved him. She could not have been happier except the "old Catholic guilt" kept revisiting her in her quiet hours. Her conscience bothered her but not enough to change the pattern of satisfying her new desire.

As the summer faded into fall, they would take short weekend trips together to remote getaways located in close proximity to Farmington. These excursions included the Four Corners area where the New Mexico, Arizona, Utah and Colorado borders came together to form the hub. At the monument, which was a large square cement slab scored into four sections representing the exact spot that the four states joined, Jas declared: "Look, I can be in four states at the same time." And with that, she placed each hand and each foot in a different state assuming a pose that looked pretty much like a twisted pretzel. Nick took a picture of her in her provocative position and stated: "This is lovely. You're going to really like it."

"Sure, that sounds pretty much like a blackmail scam to me. Name your price and have it done with."

"Oh, no. It's not going to be that easy. You must suffer for a while. I could sell it to one of the weekly rags, but then you're not a celebrity yet so it wouldn't be worth much. Perhaps I'll hang on to it and have something to hold over your head when you do become famous."

"Of course you will, you rat-bastard."

"Now, now, compliments will get you nowhere."

And with that they dissolved into laughter and, still standing in four states, they shared a hug and a fleeting kiss. A passerby offered to take a picture of them and they readily agreed. Nick handed the stranger his camera and while still hugging they posed for the picture. Jas was inspired to start a photo album of them chronologically arranging the photos in the order of the places they visited.

❦

That same autumn, they toured the Aztec Ruins National Monument located just a few miles from Farmington and wandered through the ancient structures dating back from the 11th to the 13th centuries. They were both history-nuts and thoroughly enjoyed poking around in ancient ruins. Although there was a mummy cave at the monument, Jas talked Nick out of exploring it and he was quick to oblige. Jas thought exploring death would put a damper on her new found exuberance for life and she didn't want anything to interfere with the delightful gamut of feelings she was experiencing. In concert with her new hobby, the photo album, she approached a young couple and asked if they would take a picture of Nick and her. This was another tradition that would continue throughout their relationship. The album was the thing Jas treasured most as it was a history of their lives together. She kept it on the nightstand closest to her bed and would examine it each night before falling asleep.

Before winter set in, Nick and Jas took the narrow gauge train to Silverton which left from Durango, Colorado, and returned passengers back to Durango at the end of the ride. Passing through beautiful isolated country they were enchanted by the scenery as the train traveled into the Rocky Mountains climbing toward Silverton. They were now out of the desert and into tall pines. The aspen trees were breathtaking having been transformed by the autumn frost to brilliant gold and groves of them stood out surrounded by the reds, oranges and yellows of the oak brush snuggled in among the green pines. The La Plata's snow-capped peaks could be seen in the distance adding more enchantment to the wonderful virgin landscape.

Upon reaching Silverton, the train stopped long enough for passengers to have lunch and do some shopping. The couple ate at a Mexican restaurant indulging in tamales, tacos, refried beans and ice cold beer. After lunch, Nick took Jas into a unique little shop featuring Indian jewelry some of which had been made by a local Native American vender, "Grandma Corn Blossom." Corn Blossom was well known throughout the Southwest and Nick bought Jas a fetish necklace fashioned of tiny multi-colored birds carved out of semi-precious materials such as red cornelian, tan jasper, rose quartz, green malachite, black onyx, and natural turquoise strung on a sterling silver chain, interspaced with small brown wooden beads and secured with a sterling silver clasp. Nick said, as he placed the necklace around her neck, "Primitive people believed the fetish had magical power to protect or aid its owner. It was regarded with superstition, extravagant trust, reverence and obsessive devotion. So, you now have a powerful talisman in your possession. Guard it well or you may incur the wrath of the Kachinas who are touted to be deified ancestral spirits and claimed among Indians to visit pueblos at intervals."

I will treasure this forever. Jas clutched the necklace in profound reverence. It was the first gift Nick had given her and would always be considered sacred but for more noble reasons.

❦

Mesa Verde National Park, located not too far from Farmington, was another intriguing place to explore. The park offered a spectacular insight into the lives of the ancient Pueblo Indians who reportedly lived there for 700 years, specifically from A.D. 600 to A.D. 1300. The site included, among other interesting structures and artifacts, approximately 600 cliff dwellings and kivas. The kivas were used by the ancients for religious rituals and had a place of prominence in the community. They were square-walled or rounded depending on the tribe, and were usually located underground. Nick and Jas climbed up and down the rickety ladders until they were exhausted. Even in their exhaustion, they found it almost impossible to stop because the site was so alluring and there was much to see. They finally gave up, realizing that they couldn't do it all in one visit.

❦

When not taking short trips, other pastimes included lazy afternoons lounging around the pool, hiking, canoeing down the San Juan River, local sightseeing and just relaxing and chatting about a multitude of common interests. Having already lost her heart, Jas became even more entangled in the relationship. She had never known anyone quite like Nick. He was everything she ever dreamed of. What's that old saying: "What he doesn't have, he doesn't need." She felt she had loved him even before God put the stars in the heavens.

Jas' every waking moment was punctuated with thoughts of Nick. He was the first thing she thought of upon awakening and the last thing she thought of before falling asleep. Cole Porter must have had her in mind even before she was born when he composed *Night and Day* in 1932. How accurately the words fit her situation:

"Night and day, you are the one

Only you beneath the moon or under the sun

Whether near to me, or far

It's no matter darling where you are

I think of you…"

41

CHAPTER 4

CLOUDY SKIES

Not every weekend was spent lollygagging around. The two were also somewhat preoccupied by the redecoration of Nick's mansion. Farmington, being located in the Southwest, was saturated with furniture stores and other high-end shops featuring Southwestern design. If Nick liked a particular design or style, they would obtain the name of the artisan and explore the cost of a custom-made replica usually with some desired modification. Although no artisan was ever commissioned, it was fun nonetheless to daydream. When Nick saw an item he liked that was in stock, he would always look to Jas for approval before purchasing it. She would then shake her head – not always up and down.

And, as if he needed to further prove his lack of style, Nick suggested they apply terra cotta paint throughout the mansion stating it would give it an authentic Southwestern "flavor." A stunned Jas faked a gag and told him he needed therapy. "If you paint all the rooms terra cotta, they will be considerably darker and you'll lose a lot of the rustic charm that was built in at the time of construction. Nick, I think most of your taste is in your mouth. That is really tacky."

"That's why I hired you. I know my shortcomings. I surrender. You're the visionary. From this point forward I'm your minion and will follow your lead." Pulling out his white handkerchief and waving it in the air would be a ritual that he would follow with a degree of regularity. This he adopted as his symbol of resignation.

"I do want your input. After all, you have to live here. However, I'm not going to let you make drastic mistakes that you will later regret."

Nick threw his hands up, smiled at Jas and said: "You're driving this bus. Go ahead and do what you were trained to do. I'm sure I'll love it." With that he again pulled out his crumpled handkerchief and waved it in the usual surrender mode only this time with more flurry.

❦

Nick's father had been infatuated with Kachina dolls and native pottery. Over the years he had amassed a considerable collection of both. He had a version, or two, of nearly every Kachina imaginable, some of his favorites were *Story Teller, Eagle Dancer, Mother Crow* and *Hoop Dancer*. His pottery was estimated to be worth thousands of dollars. Without exception, all of the items were extremely valuable having been purchased many years before and were increasing in value with the passage of time. Nick had them displayed helter-skelter throughout the house which made them vulnerable to impending disaster not to mention ascetically unpleasing. Jas wanted to honor his father's collection and protect the pieces from getting damaged, so she suggested he have a special

44

display case built with locked sliding glass doors in the recreation room and all of the treasures arranged together in one place. Nick readily agreed and set about building the project himself as he was rather handy when it came to woodworking, especially bookshelves and display pieces. He had a shop attached to the garage which would be the envy of any carpenter. Jas was more than impressed with the completed product. He truly was a perfectionist or was it better described as "obsessive/compulsive." The display case was etched with Southwest designs in the wood on the top brace. It was from floor to ceiling and encompassed the entire breadth of one wall. Even at that, it was barely adequate enough to hold all the items.

Helping Nick transfer his collections to the bookcase was great fun. Jas was awestruck at the workmanship that went into making the Kachina dolls. She mentally selected her favorite and fingered it lovingly. It was the *Story Teller*. The main 'character' was a happy, chubby Indian, the Story Teller, with lots of children climbing all over him. They all were laughing and having great fun. It made her happy; it was an uplifting piece. Happy and loving – not the way she remembered her own childhood when she and her sister would listen to wild and sometimes morbid bedtime stories their father told usually when he was drunk and abusive. Then there were the fights her parents would have over him being away from home days on end and coming home with the tell-tail signs of having been with another woman. Her mother had done her best to protect her daughters – even through the times when their father would disappear for days and then come home with flimsy excuses about where he had been. Those days had left their impression. That was certain! Even as a child of tender years, Jas was taught by her mother not to trust men. She could still hear her mother say: *They will only use you, abuse you and discard you when they are through with you.*

Jas loved her parents in spite of it all, but she closed off a portion of her heart that had never been opened by anyone – not even her late husband. She gently stroked the merry little Kachina as a tear slid down her cheek. Suddenly, Nick breezed into the room.

"Hey, are you still among the living?" he asked.

46

She held up the Kachina. "Oh, I'm just wondering what story is being told to cause so much joy in all these little children. This is truly lovely. Something about it has captivated my heart. We have to find a very special place for this piece."

⊙⊶⊰⊱⊷⊙

Work on the mansion was progressing and the results of every project were impressive. The easy way with which they worked together had not gone unnoticed by either of them. Each day they grew a little closer; a bit more comfortable. The intimacy was becoming more fiery and powerful. There were times Jas would look at Nick as they were working, and suddenly be overcome by this strange and terrifying feeling. That little "door" that harbored her deepest self was slowly being pried open. Nobody but Nick had ever been allowed that close. Her mother's voice continued to echo in her mind, warning her not to trust. Yes, Mother had taught her very well.

It didn't help matters that one of Nick's traits was that he liked to banter and tease, which was fine

47

until it came to his graphic descriptions of encounters with other beautiful women at the bank, grocery store, or where ever he happened to be. His intent was nothing more than to elicit a reaction from Jas. Nick put a lot of credence in jealousy. His theory was, if you weren't jealous, you really didn't care much. Jas played along, but inside a feeling clenched at her gut that made her want to run away. Her mother's voice shrieked ever louder in her ears. It began with harmless banter meant in fun, but a little feeling of suspicion and envy suddenly took shape in her mind – something black and foreboding. Jas began to feel insecure and even threatened by these other women whom she had never met. The black form she had created in her mind urged her to face herself in the mirror. She stared at the reflection with judgment and loathing convincing herself she could never measure up to these voluptuous ghosts that haunted her thinking. A satisfied man does not continue to shop, she thought bitterly. In the heat of passion and the warmth and comfort of the relationship they had built, she never considered the possibility that Nick might betray her. Infidelity was not something she could or would ever tolerate. She would not make the same mistake her mother made.

Days, weeks and months slid by and the holidays were upon them. Nick was invited to his daughter Nicole's for Thanksgiving dinner. Nicole had encouraged her father to bring someone with him if he wanted. He invited Jas and the day, needless to say, was delightful. His grandchildren were enthusiastic, energetic and extremely excited anticipating Christmas right around the corner. They immediately bonded with Jas and clung to her as the new-found grandmother. They even argued over who would sit by her at dinner. Laughingly, she said to Nick, "Look, I have a fan club." Jas and Nicole became fast friends. Although Jas was old enough to be Nicole's mother, she looked to be a contemporary and the two women were engaged in relaxed conversation as Jas assisted Nicole in the dinner preparation.

"I really love what you are doing with the villa," said Nicole, "and it is great to see Dad act alive again instead of doing nothing but managing his investments. How boring!"

Jas rolled her eyes and smiled. "That project is my dream job."

Nicole said she and her sisters had resisted the move to Farmington. Leaving life-long friends and moving to "a hick town" was inconceivable to the girls who were just approaching their teens. The move took place over the Christmas holidays which made it even more difficult. However, the girls soon learned that "a hick town" really wasn't so bad after all. "We eventually forgave Dad for uprooting us," she laughed. "It proved to be a blessing in disguise."

"Farmington is a great place to live," Jas agreed.

"I hope you get to meet my sister, Theresa. She is so much like Dad, always joking around and teasing. They *love* watching people squirm! One of these days," she threatened, "the shoe will be on the other foot. I want to be there when that happens."

"I am all too familiar with your dad's teasing," Jas added.

Nicole smiled pleasantly and picked up a beautifully arranged platter of food. "Would you mind bringing that other plate? I think we are about ready to eat."

Jas scooped up the platter and followed Nick's daughter into the dining room.

The grandchildren had decorated with purple turkeys, orange pumpkins and antiquated pilgrims appended to the sliding glass door, all contributing to the delightfully happy holiday environment. The centerpiece, a cornucopia of silk fall flowers, dried ears of corn and terra cotta colored candles complimented the table setting. Everyone sat down and shared a scrumptious turkey dinner with all the trimmings and dessert choices of pumpkin, pecan or apple pie *ala mode.* Nick's mantra was: "Life is uncertain, eat dessert first." And usually he did.

After dinner, Jas helped with the clean-up and then everyone settled in the living room. The McGregor family, all accomplished musicians, took turns playing the piano. Jas surprised everyone by taking a turn as well, playing her all-time favorite, Gershwin's *Rhapsody in Blue.* After she finished an almost perfect rendition, an astounded Nick said: "You're just full of surprises, aren't you?"

51

She smiled coyly, "If you only knew."

Nick just nodded his head, feigning surprise.

"Actually," Jas confessed "I'm a mediocre piano player, even less than mediocre. I usually manage to stumble through *Chop Sticks* or *Heart and Soul*. However, a few years back when the United States hosted the summer Olympics, a tribute was made to Gershwin. Part of the entertainment consisted of a multitude of pianos, all painted sky-blue, placed at different levels on a stage and the pianists, sporting sky-blue tuxedos and formal dresses, played *Rhapsody in Blue* in perfect unison. I was awestruck. It was so beautiful; I could have kicked myself for not recording it, but who knew? Afterwards, I bought the sheet music and practiced until I had blisters on my fingers. I finally memorized the refrain. I'm certainly not skilled enough to play all of the intricate parts of that magnificent composition. However, I can now play it, well, the refrain, anywhere anytime from memory and often do so at home to keep 'my skills honed'. Thought I'd better fess up before you asked me to play Chopin or Beethoven."

"I'm still impressed," Nick responded, "you certainly nailed it." And, with that he thought to himself what a magnificent delightful creature she is. *Who does that? Who in the hell does that?*

CHAPTER 5

COLD FRONT

A lthough Farmington was considered desert, the winters could get fairly cold – more like frigid. This winter was no exception and the weatherman predicted there would be a white Christmas if the current conditions prevailed. Jas, not having the space to go all out, limited her decorations to a nativity scene on the fireplace, an artificial wreath on the front door and a small artificial tree sparsely trimmed in the living room. Living alone was not conducive to getting very elaborate.

Nick asked her to come "lend the female touch" and help him with his decorating. He told her Theresa and her family planned to travel to Farmington to spend some time with him and Nicole and her family the week before Christmas when all the children would be on Christmas break. Nick also asked her if she would help with cooking and entertaining his guests. She readily agreed but immediately inserted a disclaimer as to her cooking skills.

"Okay," Nick responded, "we'll buy everything we can at the deli and spruce it up with salads, relishes and whatever else you think we need. I would really appreciate your help. Besides, you haven't met Theresa."

"I know, and I'm happy to assist wherever I can." And she meant it with all her heart.

Was he actually pulling her into his family circle? Or, was this a ploy to fill the void left by the departure of his live-in maid?

@⊗⊹⊗☺

Theresa's visit was twofold unbeknownst to Nick. Nicole and Theresa had secretly planned a surprise birthday party for Nick the Saturday before Christmas which was not his actual Christmas Eve birthday but worked in nicely with the weekend. Nicole recruited Jas to help pull off the surprise. Having enlisted Nick to babysit, the three women feigned a shopping trip. The deception allowed them to slip away and surreptitiously decorate the dining room at The River Side, Nick's favorite restaurant. The sisters on the sly invited all of Nick's relatives and friends and swore them to secrecy. Unfortunately, Nick's other two daughters were unable to attend, but they promised to call.

Upon arriving at the restaurant, the three women got to work stringing light blue and white (Nick's favorite color combination) crepe paper swags from the ceiling, filled the balloons and spread the dazzling white linen tablecloths. Each of the six tables was decorated with a center piece consisting of white flowers accented with blue Christmas-type balls and a blue satin ribbon. When they were finished, the three women stood back and admired their handiwork.

"I think our work is done here," said Nicole.

"It looks great! Nick will be so surprised," Jas added, gloating as they high-fived each other.

With all of the celebrating, Jas decided to do some last minute shopping for a new dress. She found exactly what she was looking for at an exclusive boutique. The dress was blue, of course, and wildly expensive. But Jas decided it was worth it. In fact, the dress was remarkably attractive. The salesclerk at the boutique suggested she purchase the matching shoes to complete the "Cinderella-look" which she did without even asking the price.

At the appointed hour, the invited guests, including Jas, congregated in the dining room of the restaurant awaiting the arrival of the guest of honor. They didn't have to wait long. Nick, flanked on each side by his two amazingly beautiful daughters, was caught totally unaware. The look on his face when the crowd roared "SURPRISE" was priceless. He then turned to his daughters and, admonishing them, said "I could have had a heart attack, you know!" They both laughed and he kissed their cheeks. As they watched, their father was whisked off to the bar to partake in liquid refreshment with some of his old friends.

"Don't be long," Nicole shouted as they left, "dinner will be served in fifteen minutes."

Nick gave her an acknowledging nod as the noisy group of men ushered him hastily into the adjoining bar. The hostesses busied themselves with seating guests. Theresa and Nicole were placed on each side of Nick at the head table. Jas was seated at one of the front tables with some of the McGregor relatives, including Nick's two aunts who would prove to be very chatty and witty dinner companions. The rest of the tables were left open to whoever wanted to sit together. A photographer walked around snapping pictures to commemorate the celebration.

Waiters in burgundy coats scurried around with steaming plates as dinner was served. Nick and entourage returned to the dining room and took their respective places. There was a pleasant hum of conversation, clinking glasses and ripples of laughter as guests plowed through dinner. Then, as though it were the final act of a Broadway production, the band struck up "Happy Birthday". Everyone swung their heads toward the door where a massive birthday cake was being wheeled in on a serving cart. The crowd clapped and cheered as Nick's daughters dragged him from his chair over to the cake where he blew out the candles. He grabbed his chest and feigned passing out. Everyone laughed and the waiters began cutting and serving the cake and ice cream.

Suddenly the band began playing *It Had To Be You*. Nick's eyes captured Jas and he immediately dabbed his mouth with a napkin and excused himself from the table. He never let her out of his gaze as he approached her table. Extending his right hand, he asked her to dance. Others were already moving in rhythm to the sweet band sounds as they stepped onto the dance floor. As Nick held Jas in his arms, he noticed how lovely she looked.

"You look amazing, my love," he whispered.

She smiled, feeling the warmth of his body as they began to glide to the music. They made a handsome couple and the other guests stopped dancing to watch. This delighted Nick as he loved being the center of attention. However, Jas suddenly felt self-conscious and could hardly wait for the dance to end.

At its conclusion, Nick escorted her back to her table and squeezed her hand transmitting a longing and a desire to be intimate. Jas sipped wine and watched as he danced with each of his daughters, and as he went from table to table dancing with all the female guests. Jas was asked to dance by several male attendees but begged off using new shoes as an excuse. As the party progressed, everyone seemed to be in high spirits and the event could not have been more enjoyable.

Around eleven the party finally dwindled down to just a few couples. Nick sat down by Jas and slid his arm around her waist.

"Theresa and her family are staying at the villa, so unfortunately, I won't be able to see you tonight. Will you come have dinner with me tomorrow evening after they leave?"

"Yes, I'd be delighted."

"My, my, so formal?"

"Just in keeping with the tone of the evening. I hope you enjoyed yourself. The girls worked so hard putting this gig together. They are truly wonderful, Nick. You're lucky to have such angels in your pocket."

"I did enjoy myself. In fact, I had a blast and I *do* know how lucky I am and not just with two lovely daughters." He looked directly into Jas' eyes and she knew who else he meant. "This was so totally unexpected. You made it even more special. You certainly 'clean up nicely,'" he teased.

"Thank you for the compliment. Hopefully I don't come across as a skagg when I'm not 'cleaned up.'"

"No, of *course* not." He hesitated and looked at her, frowning. "That was my way of saying how lovely you look tonight. Geez, woman."

At that moment Theresa joined them "What's Dad geezing about now?"

All three laughed and with that they said their farewells. Almost as fast as it began, the party was over.

Nick walked Jas to her car and softly kissed her lips. How she wanted to be with him tonight - to feel the warmth and touch of his body close to hers. All the way home *It Had To Be You* played and replayed in Jas' head. Was there *any* love song out there that didn't fit her current situation? She didn't think so. It seemed as though every song she heard now took on a special meaning. Jas sighed as she closed the condo door behind her and kicked off her shoes. She was suddenly very tired. As Jas shed her dress and crawled into bed she did so with excited expectation at the thought of being with Nick the following evening.

❦

As soon as Theresa and her family had disappeared down the driveway Nick was on the phone to Jas. "Get over here, woman! I can't stand another moment without you."

Jas and Nick spent that evening together reliving the birthday party and reveling in each other's company. They had dinner, watched television and made love. Jas felt as though she was living a dream. She now understood the concept of an "out of body" experience where nothing seemed real. One thing she did know, her love for Nick was real. The only question left to be answered was his love for her.

❦

Dan the Weatherman became everyone's hero as Christmas morning dawned with a blanket of pure white snow turning the city into an enchanted fairyland with snowflakes sparkling in the sun. Jas dreaded midnight Christmas Eve Mass. It was always too long, too late, too cold and way past her bed time. She would skip it again this year. Therefore, she arose early enough Christmas day to attend the seven-thirty Mass at Holy Trinity. The new snow made driving difficult, if not hazardous, and she said a silent prayer of thanks when she arrived at the church without incident. In spite of the weather, the church was packed to capacity and, as expected, the Christmas decorations were breathtaking. Two large evergreen trees stood sentinel on either side of the altar and were generously adorned with small white candle-like lights. An abundance of red poinsettias surrounded the base of the trees and also graced the entire breadth of the altar and along the aisles. A beautiful Nativity scene with porcelain figures was situated at the front of the church in the center of the Dias. The Mass was inspirational and insightful and Jas was once again haunted by "that old Catholic guilt."

⊙⊛⊛⊛⊙

Since Nick was spending Christmas day with Nicole and her family, Jas accepted an invitation to have Christmas dinner in Aztec with her long-time friends, Yvonne and Allen Sullivan. They would be joined by Allen's parents who were visiting from Phoenix. After Mass Jas went home, changed into more casual attire, gathered up her gifts for Yvonne and Allen and drove to Aztec. The sun was bright and warm and the snow was rapidly melting making the highway between Farmington and Aztec travel friendly.

Yvonne was an excellent cook and the house smelled like "Christmas dinner" comingled with the scent of burning cedar wood from the fireplace. The atmosphere was friendly, warm and cozy. Jas enjoyed catching up on family news with Allen's parents, Bruce and Shirley, as they had been somewhat acquainted throughout the years through Yvonne and Allen. Bruce had since retired from the telephone company and he and Shirley were living the retirees' dream, traveling the country in a luxurious RV.

After dinner and clean-up, Jas begged off and left in order to keep a prearranged rendezvous with Nick at his home. Once again she changed clothes, slipping into something less casual and tastefully sexy. On one of their weekend excursions to Durango, Nick had seen a small *Russell* brass sculpture of cowboys and horses in an art store and commented on how much he liked it. Jas contacted the store several months later and inquired about the sculpture and asked if she could obtain one. They "would be happy to order one for her," she was told and when she asked the price she was glad she was sitting down – "it's a steal at $500.00." Okay, that wasn't her idea of a "steal" but she ordered it anyway. It would look beautiful in Nick's library. When it arrived she was surprised that it was much heavier and bulkier than she expected, but she got it wrapped and was excited to give it to him.

Nick greeted her at the door with a quick kiss on the cheek and attempted to take her coat. Jas, trying not to drop the gift, was having trouble getting her arms out of the coat. She finally handed the gift to Nick and he exclaimed "Wow! What in the world is this? I already have a set of weights."

"It's your Christmas slash birthday gift. Go ahead and open it! After all, Christmas is almost over."

With that Nick, very methodically and painstakingly, unwrapped the *Russell* brass sculpture. He sucked in his breath and exclaimed:

"I don't believe it! How in the world… This is so totally unexpected."

He then placed it on the fireplace mantle and stood back to admire it. "I'm overwhelmed. Thank you so much. I know this sounds pedestrian, but you shouldn't have."

"I knew how much you liked it and besides, what do you get the man 'who has everything' and I do mean *everything*."

He knew exactly at what she was hinting and put his arm around her waist so they could admire the *Russell* together.

"Hold on, I have something for you," he said. "With all this excitement, I almost forgot."

He went to the tree and retrieved a small package and handed it to her. She was almost afraid to

66

open it not wanting to be disappointed as she was hoping for something committal, like a ring maybe. She finally mustered up the courage to unwrap the box. Inside was a beautiful gold cross pendant.

"How utterly perfect," she exclaimed, "I really love it." And she did really love it.

"Here, let's try it on; I'm glad you like it. I agonized over what to get you and decided with your religious devotion and all, a cross would be appropriate." Nick fastened the chain around her neck. From that moment, the cross would remain a permanent appendage never to be removed.

"And, drum roll maestro, if you please!" Nick turned his back for a minute, bent to get something else from under the tree and when he turned around he had the *Story Teller* adorned with red and green ribbon in his out-stretched hands. "After all, what do you get the woman 'who has everything, and I do mean *everything.*'"

Now it was Jas' turn to suck in her breath. "Oh, my God, you don't mean it. Is it really for me?"

"Yes, my dear, you love it much more than I ever could and I want you to have it. I hope it brings you as much joy and pleasure as you've brought me."

The rest of the night was indeed filled with joy and pleasure – for both!

… and so it began….

PART TWO

…and so it continues…

CHAPTER 6

GATHERING CLOUDS

The work on the mansion continued in earnest. It had gone from simple redecorating to significant remodeling and Jas spent most of her spare time with Nick. The transformation of the mansion was amazing. As the winter dissolved into spring, the relationship between Jas and Nick remained unchanged. Not that it was bad, it's just that Jas was head-over-heels in love with Nick and she hoped with all her heart to be a permanent part of his life. In that way, Jas was still an old fashioned girl. Nick had never said anything that led her to believe there would be a future together, nor did he say anything to the contrary.

That old phantom that haunted her mind had come back, this time with a vengeance. Its power over her was growing, always skulking behind her thoughts. Now when he joked about other women she became anxious about the relationship. The encounters he described were benign, if one could believe what he said. Jas, however, was beginning to question whether his intentions were to make her jealous or whether there was some other ulterior motive behind all of it. Had he just been using her all this time? Was she so blinded by love that she couldn't see it? In her ear the whispers of doubt became louder. This was just as her mother had predicted. Nick would be gone and she'd be nothing more than a vague memory – if even that.

A ripple of panic caused her to tremble. What were her choices? If she gave him up, her life would be in shambles. After the intense emotions she experienced having been with Nick, both good and bad, she knew she would never be the same without him. With every doubt – every question – the phantom created by her mother became stronger. Her mind searched for answers to allay her fears. Even though Nick had never said the words "I love you" his actions seemed to indicate he did care. Finally she resolved that as long as he continued to *show* love, she would be appeased at least for the time being. Content with that for now, she decided to remain at least until the redecoration of the mansion was completed. If nothing in Nick changed, then she would have to make that awful decision. For now, she would continue to love him and show that love just as before with the determined expectation that he would eventually reciprocate. Patience was not one of her virtues and so she prayed that the wait would be brief and in the end fruitful.

What Jas didn't know was that Nick had been pressured, or more aptly forced, to marry Stephanie. It was a day from hell when Nick received the letter from Stephanie informing him she was pregnant. He had been home on leave from the Air Force only a few days but long enough to have impregnated her. Even though he cared for her, he never really was in love with Stephanie. Nonetheless, he would tell her he loved her when they married and thereafter and more frequently after Theresa was born. After Stephanie died, Nick made a vow to himself that he would never profess his love again unless he meant it. Even if he meant it, he wouldn't say it unless he was absolutely sure.

One evening, after they had completed a small painting job, Jas had noticed Nick was not himself. He told her he wasn't feeling well. He said he was extremely tired and he had been vomiting and had stomach cramps and diarrhea most of the day. He suspected he had the flu and he asked if she would mind if he lay down for a while. Jas observed he was pale and his breathing was shallow. She determined he was indeed ill and probably needed medical attention. She wanted to take him to the hospital but he declined stating he would be all right after he rested. Jas sat nearby closely watching and she suddenly realized he was fading. After much coaxing, she finally got him into her car and took him to the emergency room at Sacred Heart Hospital.

Nick was admitted and diagnosed with a severe case of listeria. The emergency room personnel told Jas he would not have lasted the night had he not been rushed to the hospital. She was also informed there had been over two hundred deaths and thousands sickened as a result of this current outbreak. Jas remembered Nick had lunch at his favorite deli and had probably been infected there by the vegetables or fruit. Nick was dehydrated and running a high fever. For the next two days Nick remained in a semiconscious critical condition. Jas spent as much time by his side as her job and the hospital personnel would allow considering "Nurse Ratchet" ran a tight ship and enforced visiting hours with an iron fist. On the third day when Jas arrived, Nick was sitting up "enjoying lunch" which consisted of warm clear broth and Jello. Jas was so excited to see how much improved he was she couldn't control her exuberance.

"Damn you. How dare you scare me like that!" she exclaimed.

"Right. This was all contrived to upset you and test your love. I see it worked." Nick croaked.

Jas planted a kiss on his forehead, took his hand in hers and silently said a prayer of thanks. She told Nick how worried she had been and how relieved she was to see him so much improved. She then slid her hand under the sheet and slowly moved it down his torso caressing him as she did. She leaned over and whispered in his ear, "As soon as you recover I'm going to ravage your body, take you places you've never been and you're going love every second of it."

"Hummm, anticipation is part of the experience. I'm already lovin' it," was Nick's soft reply.

At that moment, the door burst opened and Nurse Ratchet briskly walked in. She could have been an actress as she never missed a cue. Jas quickly removed her hand from under the sheet but not before Ratchet surmised what was going on. "Visiting hours are *over*. You have to leave NOW."

"Okay, okay, I'm going." Jas squeezed Nick's hand and started toward the door. Nick whispered her name and she turned just as *he* blew *her* a kiss. She responded by throwing him her signature departure kiss. Once in the corridor Jas slumped against the tile hospital wall. Her knees turned to jelly as she slid down the wall into a sitting position on the floor. She wrapped her arms around her legs, buried her head in her knees and quietly sobbed tears of relief and gave thanks to God for Nick's improved condition. He had turned the corner. She could not bear to think of a life without Nick.

Nick was released from the hospital a day later upon a promise that he would have a caretaker at home to help him. Jas, of course, was that caretaker. Basically Nick was very healthy and once home he regained his strength rather quickly thanks to Jas' undivided attention. She closed her business for a week to spend with him in order to ensure he took his meds timely and in the proper dosage. She prepared healthy meals and encouraged him to eat and drink as much as he could. Nick's medications made him drowsy so he slept quite a bit cradled and snug in the knowledge he had a guardian angel watching over him – an angel that he deeply loved.

※

With Nick's extensive experience in aviation and airport administration he had been recruited by the FTA to become a board member on the Airport Commission. Nick was happy to be able to be a part of the group and had been on the board for two consecutive terms. It wasn't a huge commitment as they only met once every other month unless there was a special project.

"With plans for a new airport expansion underway," Nick told Jas, "I will have to devote more time reviewing the construction from an aviator's point of view."

Thursday afternoon Jas answered the phone. She smiled when she heard Nick's voice.

"Hi Jas! Look, honey I'm sorry to have to do this, but the Airport Commission has called a special meeting tonight so I can't make it for dinner. Forgive me?"

"Of course, but you'll have to make it up *somehow*."

Nick laughed. "I'll see what I can do. Gotta run, but I'll call you later."

Jas' girlfriends had been asking her to get together. She hardly saw them anymore so this would be a good opportunity for a girl's night out. They had a lot of catching up to do. Jas called and arranged to meet them at a quaint little café where they could enjoy dinner then catch a movie at the new big screen theater in downtown Farmington. The girls parked in a public lot and walked the short distance up Main to the theater. It had been a fun evening with lots of laughter as they lined up on the sidewalk outside the theater ticket window. There were numerous boutiques, a gourmet culinary store, a frozen yogurt and ice cream shop and some upscale restaurants along Main.

Jas, was last in line to purchase her ticket, when the sound of a familiar laugh caught her attention. She glanced over her shoulder as she crammed her change into her purse. The smile melted from her face. To her shock, there was Nick leaving the restaurant with the woman from Carlson Realty. For a moment Jas was too stunned to speak. They appeared pretty chummy as they walked toward her car parked just a block away. Cheryl followed Jas's gaze and frowned.

"Say, Jas, isn't that McGregor over there? Wonder who he's with. My, my, his wife was a 'movie star.' He certainly has slipped." She shook her head.

Jas felt a tight knot form in her gut. All of her doubts and pent up emotions made her tremble and she tried to hold back her tears. This was not the place to fall apart – here in front of her friends. How could Nick lie and betray her like that? Even worse, Carlson was

78

married. She guessed they could cover by claiming she was "entertaining" a client.

It was common knowledge that the Carlsons had made a financial killing in the real estate market before it collapsed. After the collapse they made another killing buying foreclosed properties and then reselling them and offering their own financing. Looking back, Jas remembered seeing a Lexus bearing a Carlson Realty logo on its door panels exiting the Desert Rose Estates where Nick lived. This happened on more than one occasion. The two cars would pass each other at about the same location at about the same time most evenings. Did Nick perhaps have another "contract"! Anger and confusion made her put her fingers to her temples as if that would somehow quell the turbulence in her mind and heart. Should she cut her losses and boogie or should she hold out hope that he would eventually return her love? Her mind said "go" but her heart said "no." Heart wins every time!

It was mid-summer and the San Juan County Board of Commissioners staged their annual Law Enforcement Appreciation Banquet to honor law enforcement personnel with five, ten, fifteen, twenty and twenty-five years of service or more. This was an elaborate formal dinner dance and all of law enforcement received invitations as well as the local merchants who supported LE during the year. Jas had attended the affair in the past with casual friends and she liked dressing up and going out so she asked Nick if he would accompany her. She expected him to decline knowing how much he disliked "those kinds of things." Much to her surprise, he accepted. She had waited until the day before the event to muster up the courage to ask and upon his acceptance Jas had to scurry to get ready. She selected a knee-length spaghetti strapped satin dress with a sweeping skirt of ivory chiffon. Nick had a tuxedo and he relished wearing it knowing how handsome he looked, that is if he interpreted the glances from the opposite sex correctly – which he usually did.

When the day of the dinner dance arrived Nick called Jas at work, "Honey, something has come up that I must attend to. I won't be able to pick you up but I will meet you there. I don't anticipate being too late. Save me a seat."

Jas was disappointed but her voice never betrayed her. She couldn't help but wonder what kind of "emergency" had come up this time to demand his immediate attention. More red flags. *Where there's smoke, there's fire.* Jas was confused and tormented as the dark phantom rose in her mind yet again.

The event always had a large turnout and the banquet hall was crowded when Jas arrived. She found an empty table in front close to the bandstand. An old friend Jas had dated several years before came over and sat down in the chair Jas was saving for Nick.

"Jas, how are you? How nice to see you."

"Hello, Brandon. Nice to see you as well. How have you been?" As she chatted with Brandon, her eyes kept watching the door for Nick. She finally spotted him and waved as he came in. Nick smiled and strode across the room and sat down on the other side of Brandon. Jas introduced them and they shook hands.

"I hope I'm not intruding," said Brandon. He could see that Jas was uncomfortable.

"Of course not," Nick assured him. "You are more than welcome to join us if you'd like."

"That is very kind," said Brandon looking around. "But I'm here with a date and need to get back to my table or I will be in big trouble." He smiled as he got up.

"Jas, great to see you and it was a pleasure meeting you, Nick."

As Brandon, left Jas stared at Nick for a moment. The voice in her head was taunting her again, suggesting that perhaps Nick was trying to make it appear that she was not his date. She tried not to listen and made conversation as dinner was served.

Suddenly Nick whistled softly and spoke under his breath to no one in particular, "Hello Baby, where have you been all my life?" Jas put down her fork and followed Nick's gaze to the table opposite theirs and recognized Shelly Lyons looking absolutely ravishing in a red satin gown, her fabulous blond hair swept into a very becoming up do. Jas then observed the back of Tom Lyons as he left his table heading toward the bar she surmised to get a drink for Shelly and him. They obviously had just arrived. Tom and Shelly were condo-dwellers and shared the same complex as Jas so Jas knew them and was actually good friends with the couple. Shelly had become a confident of sorts. She knew Jas was seeing someone but didn't know the details.

After all that had taken place during the evening and in the recent past with Nick, Jas had reached her limit. Nick's comment just reiterated his disrespect for her feelings. She knew his comment was for her benefit. Irked, Jas got up and walked over to Shelly's table. A very surprised Nick followed her every move with his eyes. Jas greeted Shelly and sat down in Tom's chair. Without looking toward Nick, Jas told Shelly that Nick was wondering "where she'd been all his life," and she told Shelly she suspected he wanted to meet her. Shelly looked surprised as she knew Jas knew she was married. Shelly raised her eyebrows in a questioning gesture to which Jas immediately replied, "He's my date or whatever sitting directly opposite you with his eyes bulging. I'm leaving since I'm not feeling well and thought you might want to introduce yourself to him. His name is Nick 'Rat-Bastard' McGregor." Shelly immediately connected the dots and nodded comprehension. As Jas started to get up, Shelly took her arm and said, "Honey, you stay put. Someone is going to get his come-uppance. Tell Tom I'll be right back. You go ahead and drink my margarita if you like. I have a job to do."

Jas, not wanting to miss the "come-uppance" stayed put. Shelly rose, adjusted her gown, ran her hand up her neck smoothing the up do, took a deep breath, squeezed Jas' shoulder and sauntered toward Nick. Nick, taking all of this in, was transfixed. He didn't know what to think or expect. Shelly approached and, leaning over Nick, whispered in his ear: "Nicky, would you dance with me?" Nick was stunned and flattered. The two walked to the dance floor and Nick took Shelly in his arms in a close dance stance. Shelly stated, "Oh, Nicky, I can hardly breathe, but that's okay because what I have to say is for your ears only." Nick was unsure what to think and glanced in Jas' direction as if to ask "What do I do now?" Shelly, whispered to him as they danced, "I trust you realize that your date is one of the most beautiful women I've ever known, both inside and out, and there you are scouring the room ogling other women." Nick then realized that his "make Jas jealous" routine had backfired and had spiraled out of control. Not knowing what else to do he kept dancing. Shelly continued, "As for me, I know your kind. Need I say more? I think you've just burned your last bridge with Jas. You've thrown Aladdin's Lamp back into the ocean and you have no idea what you've lost." With that Shelly pulled away from Nick and walked off the dance floor leaving him to deal with the embarrassment. However, before she got too far, she turned and said, "Oh, by the way, I hope you enjoy the rest of your evening. We're leaving." She went back to her table and the three of them, Shelly, Tom and Jas, left the banquet hall. Jas never looked back. Once outside she asked Shelly to tell her what happened. Shelly reiterated the conversation and Jas, unsure of her feelings, was already rethinking her strategy. Something inside her, however, jumped with joy. *It's about damn time. Now he knows how it feels.*

Nick stood there for a moment trying to comprehend what had just happened as he watched them depart. He had come here for Jas and now she was furious at him. More than being embarrassed he was horrified that his teasing and clowning around may well

85

have cost him the future with the woman he loved more than life itself. He hurried out to the parking lot and hit the speed dial on his cell with Jas's number. No response. He called her the next day. No response. When he got no response the third day he decided to seek her out. He had had time to ponder his ill-advised actions and the potential consequences. He waited until she had returned home from work and arrived just as she did. She was thus unable to avoid him.

I was insensitive and wrong thought Nick. *I need to make it up to her if it isn't too late. I never intended to hurt her. She's too sensitive and I'm too insensitive – what a dangerous combination.*

When Jas drove up, Nick was standing outside his car leaning against the passenger door. She exited her vehicle and started toward her front door without looking in his direction. Nick caught up to her, took her arm and gently turned her toward him. He took her in his arms and said, "Jas, I am so sorry I hurt you. I didn't mean to. That's just something guys do, you know, look at pretty women. I realize now how insensitive I was. Give me another chance and I will never hurt you like that again." Then after a short pause, he added: "Besides, I don't want to tangle with that Shelly woman ever again." That little comment broke the ice and they laughed and cried at the same time. Jas hugged Nick and replied, "Okay, Nick, one more chance." And she made a silent promise to herself: *Only one more chance, then it's over forever.*

Once again things returned to "normal," except, that is, for Nick's discernible attitude adjustment.

…and so it continued…

PART THREE

…and so it ends…

CHAPTER 7

SEVERE STORMS

June in Farmington provided a prelude to the expected blistering hot summer. It did not disappoint. Jas was grateful she had access to a private swimming pool and took advantage of it at every opportunity. Her suntan was coming along nicely but Nick, having tanned the previous several summers, had instant tan in just a few weeks. *Wouldn't you just know, even the sun gods favor him,* thought Jas.

Work continued on the remodel and their personal situation improved but not all to Jas' liking. Nick "threw her a few crumbs" now-and-then. Jas reined in her desire to pour out the dammed up reservoir of love she was feeling and played it cool letting him take the lead. She never again told him that she loved him. She felt self-conscious when she did because he never responded in kind leaving her to wonder exactly how he felt about her. *Woman does not live on bread and water alone!*

Nick, in the past, had reacted favorably to Jas' declaration of love for him. He missed her saying so and wondered if her feelings had changed. She still had love in her eyes and expressed love through her body language, but she would never say she loved him. He was gradually beginning to realize how much he loved her. Nick knew his life would be empty without Jas. But he still couldn't say the three little words Jas so desperately wanted to hear.

෴

As the summer progressed, Jas continued to observe with regularity the silver Lexus with Carlton Realty logos on the door panels exiting the estates where Nick lived at the same time she was entering. It struck her as being odd that they would encounter each other as often as they did and always at the same time and usually at the same place. She even asked Nick if he knew to whom the car belonged. He stated he had no clue and didn't remember ever having seen such a vehicle.

More red flags. That was a blatant lie. Jas thought back to the evening she had seen Nick and Adell Carlton leaving the restaurant together confirming Nick knew Carlton. Why would he lie about it unless he had something to hide.

As July loomed hot and dry, the desert continued to wilt from the excessive heat. Even the most resilient foliage was beginning to dry up. Jas had to marvel, however, at the tenacity of the cacti and its stubborn insistence on surviving in such a hostile environment. One could look in any direction and see the heat waves rise. Even the lizards were seeking cover.

The end of July marked the one year anniversary of Jas and Nick's relationship or whatever it was. She wondered if it was the same for Nick as it was for her. But because Jas was a romantic at heart, she decided to make their one-year anniversary a memorable one anyway. She set about planning a celebration for the two of them consisting of a special dinner including champagne and appetizers to begin with, followed by a salad, a main course of grilled steak and baked potato, topped off with their all-time favorite, Ben and Jerry's ice cream. She also spent a whole afternoon shopping for a "special" outfit and found a perfect baby-pink knee-length dress with a halter top. The cut of the dress emphasized her slim figure with a bit of cleavage. Several clerks told her she looked absolutely stunning. How could she ignore "absolutely stunning?" She bought it knowing full well that clerks went to "flattery school" and that their ploy-in-trade was to make the customer feel beautiful and unable to resist the purchase. Whether ploy or no ploy, it worked!

Saturday, July 21 was not their actual anniversary date. July 24 was but the preceding Saturday appeared to be the better day to celebrate. Jas started dinner preparations and when far enough along, she changed into her new outfit. Nick was on the patio fussing with the grill in order to get the steaks started when Jas approached.

"WOW!" he exclaimed. Nick seemed genuinely to be at a loss for words as he drank in the lovely vision before him. He finally managed to say "Where did you come from and what did you do with Jas?" With that she twirled to give him the full view of the halter top back and looked back over her bare shoulder in a coquettish-way batting her long eyelashes and smiled a sweet smile that held a forbidden promise.

"Let's forget dinner and get straight to the main event," he purred.

"Not a bit of it," Jas protested, "I've slaved over a hot stove for at least five minutes and we're going to indulge in my efforts."

The evening was glorious and the dinner never more delicious. Jas was happy in an apprehensive way. She experienced new feelings coming from Nick that she couldn't identify or explain as nothing monumental had really happened. It was just his mannerisms or something she couldn't quite describe.

She caught him looking at her with "different eyes." Her anxiety was still holding her captive.

I wonder what's going on in his head, Jas thought. *Is it the wine or is something really happening or is it my imagination?*

After dinner, they sat on the swing on the patio. The evening was becoming cooler as it did in the desert and they held hands in silent appreciation. When Jas finally said it was time to clean up, Nick went with her into the kitchen.

As Jas was gathering up the dishes, Nick walked up to her and taking her by the hand said: "You know how much I value and respect your opinion. I want you to be the first to know I've fallen deeply in love with someone very special and I intend to ask her to marry me. I know now she's all I've ever wanted. She's beautiful, intelligent, a joy to be with and I feel she loves me as much as I love her. I'd be a fool to let her slip through my fingers. I have a ring and I'd like your take on it before I give it to her. I want everything to be perfect."

Nick then slipped his hand into his shirt pocket to retrieve the ring.

Jas just stared at Nick in wild-eyed disbelief. Her face contorted into something almost unrecognizable. He looked at her expression and drew back in shock. What had gone wrong? Suddenly the reality of the moment hit him like a fist to the gut. After all they had been through – all they had shared he was certain she would see through his ruse. Certainly she would know this was meant for her – that she was the woman with whom he wanted to share his life.

As thoughts tumbled through his mind, Jas whirled away from him and planted both hands on the edge of the counter as though she was about to topple over. Suddenly everything seemed to move in slow motion. Her head fell back as an anguished cry ripped the air. Deep, pitiful sobs made her shoulders quake. Her mother had been right all along. *Never trust a man.* Her limbs trembled and anguish roiled in the pit of her stomach. "Nick!" she screamed. I loved you!"

"Jas, honey…? Let me explain." He was suddenly afraid for her.

His voice sounded like a distant echo – some tiny indistinguishable din in the back of her mind. The man she loved wanted another. Why couldn't it have been her? Why hadn't he told her there was someone else in the picture? Suddenly the question screamed through her mind – *WHY? WHY? WHY?* Her stomach clenched into a tight knot; her breath came in short and irregular gasps and her face reflected the fiery explosion within. In a moment of uncontrolled grief and rage, her hand snatched up the knife on the counter and she swung around facing Nick.

"Why-y-y-y…?" Her anguished scream shattered the air again.

He could only stare, his mouth open. How could he have been such a fool? At that same moment a sick realization washed over Nick and he rushed toward to her, his arms reaching out for Jas – his precious Jas.

In a heartbeat their fate was sealed. The knife was suddenly engorged in his torso, buried nearly to the hilt. He gasped in shock and fell to his knees clutching his chest, his shirt rapidly turning crimson. He looked at her with a strange expression, his lips fighting to form words. He slowly fell forward pushing the knife deeper into his chest. As he hit the floor, the ring rolled from his hand. Jas stared at it for a moment then gingerly plucked it from the floor. Twisting the ring in her fingers, she read the inscription on the inside: "*Jas, Luv U 4-Ever, Nick.*"

Another cry erupted from the depth of her being. She crouched beside Nick, praying and hoping there would be another chance. *He loved me! Why did he never tell me…?* Everything became surreal. In her confusion she unconsciously slipped the ring onto her finger. She looked down at Nick, blood seeping from the wound and forming a widening pool on the floor where he lay.

Have I killed the only man I ever loved? What am I to do?

She frantically grabbed the phone and dialed 911 hoping against hope she was not too late to save him. After making the call, Jas knelt down beside Nick cradling him in her arms and praying. *Please God. Please don't let him die. Please don't let him die, I didn't mean to do it. Please forgive me. Nick, I love you. I love you…*

The sirens grew closer as the emergency vehicles screamed into the driveway. Jas stayed where she was as the EMTs converged on the house. She answered their calls and they followed her voice to the kitchen where she crouched on the floor holding Nick. He was bleeding profusely. Gently taking her by the shoulders, they maneuvered her out of the way and began working on him.

"I'm afraid we're too late," said one of the EMTs as he searched for a pulse. The other who was attaching an intravenous tube to Nick's arm responded: "I'm afraid you're right. He has lost a lot of blood. Let's get rolling."

Oh, God, please, please, please.... Jas thought as she stood by watching in hopeful silence. *It seems like my whole life I've managed to destroy the good things that come my way. I didn't mean for this to happen! Will God ever forgive me?*

The police arrived just as the EMTs wheeled Nick out. The police immediately segregated Jas in another room and began what some would refer to as an interview and others as an interrogation. Jas worked for attorneys the summer after she graduated college. She knew not to make any statements or answer any questions until she consulted an attorney so she invoked her constitutional right to remain silent and, upon doing so, was not questioned further. She also knew this would add to the air of suspicion already surrounding her but she had no recourse. Her first inclination was to confess but having time to reconsider as the EMTs worked over Nick, she reasoned her confession would not bring Nick back and she was not into self-sacrifice that would serve no purpose. She needed time to think; to create a scenario that would sound plausible. Deception was not her thing. However, she had never been in this position before. If ever she could conjure up a plausible story it was now. She was in a survival mode and literally in a life-death struggle. For now, silence would be the better part of valor.

Jas was taken to the police station and placed in an interrogation room. Because she exercised her right to confer with a lawyer, the detectives ceased questioning her further and allowed her the obligatory one phone call. During that summer working for attorneys, Jas became intrigued with criminal law and continued to follow interesting cases closely. Because of this, she knew who the best and brightest criminal lawyer in the area was so she contacted Samuel Morton. When "Salty" arrived at the police station he was given access to Jas in the interrogation room. Putting his finger to his lips, he cautioned her not to speak indicating the room was wired and anything that was said was probably being recorded. Salty then took out a yellow legal pad and began to write a series of questions to which Jas responded also in writing:

Q.   Have you made any kind of statement to authorities whether EMTs or law enforcement?

A.   No. I immediately asked for an attorney. They told me I wasn't under arrest at that time and they were just trying to piece together the details of what happened. I did not make a statement; I gave no explanations or any other information to anyone. Did he… did he die?

Q.   Yes, he died at the scene. He didn't make it to the hospital.

Jas collapsed into uncontrollable sobbing upon hearing that Nick actually died. Salty placed his hand on Jas' shoulder and patiently waited for her to regain control of her emotions. While Salty was waiting for access to Jas' interrogation room, the detectives had told him that Jas would be detained at the request of the DA at least until the initial investigation was concluded. He wrote:

> Q. It appears you have become a suspect so you'll be processed into the jail tonight. How are you involved?

Thinking quickly knowing suspicion would be elevated if anyone suspected a relationship between her and Nick, Jas answered:

> A. He commissioned me to remodel his home. I own an interior design shop downtown. He graciously suggested we do his remodel evenings and weekends leaving me free to run my one-man shop during business hours. I was to meet

him at his home around six or six-thirty to show him some swatches and paint samples. I found him like that, tried to revive him and immediately called 911 for help.

Q.   What did you say when you called 911?

A.   I said a man had been stabbed and needed medical assistance.

Q.   When you arrived, did you notice anything unusual?

A.   Not really unusual. It looked like someone was cleaning up after dinner. There were dirty dishes in the sink and the dishwasher was open. I was in such a state that there could have been an elephant in the kitchen and I wouldn't have noticed it.

Salty then whispered: "That's enough for now. I'm going to check on advisement and bond. You can be held for 72 hours without being charged. Since it's the weekend, you will not have your first appearance in court until Monday. Everything depends on what the DA decides to do. Don't hold out any hope of getting a bond under a million dollars as that's the going rate on a murder charge. Do you want me to contact anyone before this hits the papers?"

"My God, a million dollars! I couldn't even come up with ten thousand. Yes, please contact my close friend, Yvonne Sullivan. She lives in Aztec." Jas scribbled Yvonne's phone number on Salty's legal pad. "Let her know what happened and tell her I'm all right – for now anyway. Would you keep her apprised of the developments since I probably won't have access to the outside world for a while?"

Salty checked the phone number and said to Jas, "Yes, I'll keep in touch with Yvonne. You'll be processed into jail tonight. Tomorrow morning I will come see you first thing. In the meantime, just maintain your silence and composure. Are you okay?"

"Am I okay? No, I'm *not* okay." And with that she began to sob again.

Salty, regretting asking such an ill-advised question and feeling helpless, placed his legal pad in his brief case and left again promising to return the next day. The matron ushered a handcuffed Jas to a waiting jail transport vehicle that resembled an animal control cage on wheels.

❦

Jas was transported to the San Juan County Jail and given an orange jumpsuit and some rubber sandals, the usual jail garb. Her personal effects were confiscated and placed in a manila envelope with her identifying information written on it. It was then she remembered she had slipped the ring on her finger and was terrified that someone would notice the inscription. She toyed with the gold cross Nick had given her for Christmas as she had never removed it from the time he placed it around her neck. She hesitated taking it off asking if she could keep it and was told no. She reluctantly gave it up but kissed it before she handed it to the jail matron charged with collecting her personal belongings.

There seemed to be a lot of confusion in the booking area since it was Saturday night and a more-than-normal number of arrests were being processed. Jail personnel were stretched to the limit and arrestees were being fingerprinted and booked as fast as possible. Jas was thankful that no one took time to really look at her personal belongings, especially the inscribed ring. They were entered in the log as one Seiko ladies watch, a gold/diamond ring, a pair of gold earrings and a gold cross pendant. After she was fingerprinted and photographed she was provided a blanket and some toiletries and led to a cold sterile cell where she was locked up, sequestered from the rest of the jail population.

She sat on her bunk burying her head in her hands and sobbing. She had difficulty catching her breath and vomited into the stainless steel toilet bowl. Exhausted, she collapsed on the cold hard cot and fell into a fitful sleep fraught with dreadful dreams and a deep pain within.

When she was awakened in the morning by the jailers, she couldn't immediately remember where she was or what had happened. Then it all came back like a freight train rolling over the top of her. She was taken from her cell to the shower area and was left alone. She turned on the shower and began washing off what remained of Nick's dried blood. Sobbing, she sank to her knees on the cement shower floor and tried to grab the blood-stained water spiraling down the drain.

What have I done? What have I done?

⚜

Jas was still not allowed to mingle with the other inmates. Her breakfast was brought to her cell. Even if she had felt like eating, the bill-o-fare would have turned her off: gummy oatmeal, cold coffee and burned toast. Everything was served on cheap plastic trays with cheap plastic utensils designed to prevent suicides she surmised. She immediately had the urge to vomit again and pushed the tray as far from her as she could. She then curled up on the hard cot and covered her eyes with her arm trying to remember the string of events that culminated in her being there. She didn't want to think of it as murder. To her, murder was the willful planning and taking of somebody's life. She didn't want Nick out of her life. Just the opposite, she wanted to spend her life with him. When she thought he was pushing her away and marrying someone else she couldn't cope with it. That's when she lost control of her senses and stabbed him. *Oh, God, how could I have done that? I don't understand. I loved him and still love him with my whole being. This has got to be a nightmare. If only I could awaken and have things the way they were before I killed him. If only he hadn't been such a bastard and tormented me so much with other women. If only I had had more trust in him. If only he would have expressed his true feelings for me and not have left me to my own devices. If only, if only, if only...* She was up vomiting again.

Later that morning, Salty was escorted into her cell by a jailer. After the jailer left, Salty once again asked her how she was doing. This triggered more uncontrollable sobbing. Salty stood watching her waiting patiently until she was able to regain her composure. When she calmed down, he sat down beside her and began to ask questions but only after cautioning her that the cell had ears.

"Jasmine, tell me what happened."

"I don't know what happened before I got there, Sam, I found him like that."

Jas preferred using the name Sam rather than Salty and did so from that day on.

"Did you say anything to the EMTs when they arrived?"

"No."

"Did you say anything to the police? Anything at all?"

"No."

"Explain to me exactly what happened from the time you left your house until you arrived at his house."

"I left my house around 6:30 p.m. I always called him before I left to make sure he would be there when I arrived. He answered and told me to come. I didn't live far from him so it didn't take very long to get there. However, I did notice that same car with the Carlton Realty logos on the door panels that I previously told you about coming out of the Desert

Rose Estates. It happened quite often and I wouldn't be at all surprised if it came from Nick's residence."

"Okay, you say you encountered 'that same car' often when you were going to his house. Can you describe the car?"

"I'm not very good when it comes to makes or models but I think it was a Lexus, silver in color with the Carlton Realty logos on the door panels."

"Can you describe the driver?"

"Somewhat. She had 'dish water' blonde hair, straight and stringy. She appeared to be short and chubby from what I could tell just by looking through the windshield. Not a very attractive woman!"

"Did you travel the same route each time you went there?"

"Yes, there is only one main access road unless you want to take the long way around.

"Did you always go there at the same time of day?"

"It depended on when I got home from my shop. Sometimes I would stay late to meet with customers who work a normal work day. This didn't happen very often but I always try to accommodate potential clients.

I need the business and the goodwill. I've concluded there was no rhyme or reason to the encounters with the car. It happened so often that it made me wonder, as I've said, if she was with him and left as soon as I called. That makes the most sense to me."

"Why would he care if you knew he was with someone? Were you romantically involved?"

"Well, don't you think it would be awkward at best to have me there while he was 'entertaining' another woman since I needed his input regarding my suggestions on the changes he was making? Maybe she was married and he was having a covert affair with her."

"So, whatever the circumstances, he was obviously hiding something," said Salty.

Salty sensed Jas was not telling the complete truth and he thought the dead man must have been a complete idiot if he hadn't seen this intelligent, sensual woman for what she was and not have a romantic interest in her. Even in her disheveled state, Jas was captivating. Salty perceived that Jas and Nick had been romantically involved and hence the reason Jas had been evasive.

"How did you usually proceed when you went to his place?"

"What do you mean?"

"Okay, you drove to his house, then what?"

"The door was always locked so I knocked. He was expecting me and would let me in. Sometimes during the day, when the light was best, he would have painted areas that we had agreed on. If I had swatches or paint samples or accent pieces that I'd collected to bring, we would go over the placement of these items in the rooms where they would be used. We were never in a hurry to complete the work. He was deliberate and took his time making decisions. Remodeling can be expensive, especially if the clients keep changing their minds.

"Then what?"

"Then what, what? Then I would leave and go home. On the weekend our routine varied but during the week it almost never fluctuated."

"And this weekend…."

"This weekend we planned to work some around six or six-thirty Saturday evening. I had plans later so I dressed for a late dinner before I left home."

111

"Was anyone else included in this 'late dinner'?"

"I'd rather not say."

"It will probably become important."

Jas just remained silent and nervously bit her nails. Salty was growing skeptical by the minute and somewhat frustrated. After all, he was her lawyer and what she told him constituted privileged communication.

"Okay, for now. Tell me exactly, and I mean exactly, what happened from the time you drove up to his house until you were brought to the police station."

"I turned into the estates and, as I said before, I saw the Carlton Realty car leaving. I could not tell where it came from since we were on the main thoroughfare and not in any specific driveway."

"Did you mention the car to the police?"

"No, I didn't make any statements."

"Okay, go on."

"I drove up to Nick's house and knocked on the door. When I knocked, the door gave a few inches. That was odd because, as I said before, he always kept the door locked. He lives in an upscale neighborhood and is conscious that he could be a target for a break in. I went in and called to him but he didn't answer. I thought then that possibly he had unlocked the door for me and that he was in the bathroom or otherwise 'indisposed'. I called to him again but received no response. I went through the living room and as I walked past the kitchen I saw him laying there in a pool of blood."

"Okay, take your time, I know this is difficult."

Trying to maintain control of her emotions, Jas said in a shaky voice, "I ran to him and gently turned him over because he was laying face down. That's when I saw the knife sticking out of his chest. I was so distraught I didn't know what to do. I remember thinking that if I got the knife out it would help so I tried to pull the knife out of his chest. I could not budge it. I was instantly covered with Nick's blood from a large pool on the floor and from having cradled him in my arms as I tried to get the knife out. He was warm and I had hope that he was still alive. I even thought I detected some breathing. I reached up and grabbed the phone off the counter and dialed 911. I stayed in that position until help arrived, talking to him, encouraging him to hang on. Everything is pretty much a blur from the time I saw him there and even until now. How did all of this happen? How can I be a suspect? All I tried to do was help him."

Salty believed that Jas had not caused Nick's death. At least this part of her story was convincing. After all, what would her motive have been? She did have means and opportunity but no motive, that is, unless they were involved in some kind of romantic relationship and the green-eyed monster reared its ugly head. He was still skeptical about their involvement. The Carlson Realty car, however, spiked his curiosity. That was a lead worth pursuing. Perhaps the driver thereof was the real killer. He understood why his client at this point was the most likely suspect and why the authorities would be devoting their efforts in building a case against her.

CHAPTER 8

TURBULANCE

Monday morning dawned bright and sunny. Jas' hearing was scheduled for 9:00 a.m. before the Honorable Clarence Ratkliffe, known as the hanging judge by those who were destined to appear before him. The good thing about having a first appearance before Rats – his   nickname in the legal community – was that the case would in all probability be assigned to another judge for future hearings and trial. Although Rats was a district court judge, he was covering for the county court judges attending a judicial conference in Santa Fe and was conducting the first appearance advisements on their cases pending their return. The likelihood of him assigning himself Jas' case was little to none especially since the case against Jas had not yet been officially filed by the prosecution. Jas' first appearance before the court was the result of her having been incarcerated as a murder suspect over the weekend. Salty didn't have much hope of getting a bond set since the potential charge would be first degree murder. Upon learning that Rats would be conducting advisement hearings, any glimmer of hope Salty might have had was quickly dissipated.

Jas appeared in court as scheduled and sat at the defense table with Salty. She looked haggard with dark circles under red eyes. Her hair was carelessly pulled up in a ponytail and she was pale and listless. The bright orange jail jumpsuit exaggerated her paleness. Salty was shocked at how much she had deteriorated since he last saw her – less than twenty-four hours before. He took her hand in an attempt to reassure her but she did not respond and her whole body was limp.

After the usual courtroom prehearing routine, the judge read Jas her rights and asked if she understood them to which she responded with a weak "Yes." Salty asked the court to address bond. Rats stated that since the potential charge was a capital offense, he would not be setting bond. He then transferred the case to the next judge on the list, the Honorable Wedge Ralston, for future hearings and trial. Salty was relieved that Rats would not be the presiding judge. Judge Ralston was a no-nonsense judge but fair and reasonable.

After the hearing, Salty met with Jas in one of the stoic courthouse conference rooms and said to her, "Hang in there; we've just begun to fight." Jas nodded her head indicating that she understood. She was then led away by one of the jailers. Upon leaving the courthouse, the first thing Salty did was file an Entry of Appearance with the court with a copy to the district attorney. Having filed said document, he was entitled to request all discovery which consisted of police reports and copies/descriptions of any and all physical evidence. The prosecution was bound by law to provide the defense with any materials, reports, photographs or other evidence that pertained to the case. Failure to knowingly not do so would be a violation of the rules of criminal procedure and open the door for a mistrial or sanctions by the court. Salty then went back to his office to begin the preparation of Jas' defense. He was in his element. This is what he was born to do. It was in his DNA. He approached the challenge with excited anticipation.

◎◎◎✦◎◎◎

An arraignment hearing was set for Wednesday before Judge Ralston at which time the prosecution was required to file charges and the court would address bond. Since Jas had constant contact with most of the employees who worked in and for the judicial system, in order to avoid a conflict of interest or the appearance of impropriety, a special prosecutor was appointed by the Chief Judge. The case was assigned as a special prosecution to the Bernalillo County District Attorney's Office in Albuquerque. However, all hearings and trial would be held in San Juan County. Judge Ralston did not see the need to recuse himself as he had had little or no personal contact with Jas. If the defense and/or prosecution did not object, he would remain on the

118

case. Neither side objected. Officially, then, the Honorable Wedge Ralston would be the presiding judge in the case of *The People of the State of New Mexico v. Jasmine Zachary.*

Matthew Jacoby, the San Juan County Assistant District Attorney, handled the arraignment for the special prosecutor who was unavailable due to such short notice. The special prosecutor had determined what charges would be filed and had the paperwork prepared and faxed to Farmington for the arraignment hearing on the Monday following Jas' arrest the previous Saturday. Jacoby handed Salty a copy of the charging document as soon as Salty entered the courtroom and before the hearing began in order to give the defense time to review the charges. Salty scanned the document with a poker face. As anticipated, the prosecution had filed the highest possible charges: one count of first degree murder and one count of second degree murder. The prosecution also filed a third count: assault with a deadly weapon. The charges were class one, two and three felonies, respectively. The first degree murder charge carried a life sentence or the death penalty upon conviction. However, the prosecution had not indicated whether it would be asking for the death penalty. It was apparent the prosecution had not made that decision yet. In Salty's mind, the circumstances did not warrant the death penalty.

Jas was seated at the defense table looking somewhat better although the strain of the last few days was still clearly visible on her face and in her eyes. Salty reviewed the charges with her. She registered no noticeable reaction. Court was called to order and Judge Ralston read Jas her rights again and asked if the defense desired the complaint document read aloud. The defense said they did not. The judge then asked for motions. Jacoby announced that he had none at that time. However, when Salty requested that bond be set, Jacoby objected stating that the accused would be considered a flight risk. Salty countered that Ms. Zachary had her own business, and owned property in the area and had no criminal history. It was not likely, he argued, that she would flee. The judge listened and at the conclusion of the arguments, agreed to set bond. As it turned out, it didn't matter because bond was set at a million dollars. Jas did not have the means to come up with the ten percent required by a bondsman to post bail so it was a moot point. Jas was destined to stay in jail until at least the preliminary hearing.

◎◈◈◈◎

Jordan Slater, Salty's "Della Street" had been working in the judicial system for over twenty years as a paralegal, investigator, secretary, and basically "Jill of All Trades." Jordan was a computer whiz and could effectively run any program thrown at her without trouble or delay and Salty marveled at her tenacity, speed and skill. Jordan had not had any formal training on the use of computers. However, her talent was innate. The more difficult and challenging, the better. Jordan was the quintessential one-woman show and a breed apart. Salty had no need for any other clerical help while she was still around and he compensated Jordan handsomely for all the hats she wore.

Jordan was an attractive feisty woman in her late forties. Her black hair was cropped short and she couldn't be bothered with "girlie things" like make up and artificial finger nails. She was all natural. Her "uniform" consisted of slacks and flat heeled shoes. She wasn't concerned about being stylish but was always "office appropriate".

Jordan's biker boyfriend, Dave Jennings, hung around the office when he wasn't working as a UPS driver. He was an ex-law enforcement officer and quasi-investigator. Because of his uncanny resemblance to the oriental god Buddha, he was nicknamed *Buddha,* which was okay with him as it inferred deity. Salty hired him on an *ad hoc* basis to interview witnesses, run errands and make deliveries whenever he was available. Buddha relished working for Salty. His assignments were usually interesting and he was able to utilize his law enforcement training and experience by doing interviews and investigation. When he was required to make runs to the courthouse to file or pickup paperwork, he would almost always run into one of his past law enforcement confederates and avail himself of the opportunity to catch up on the latest gossip and determine which way the winds of public opinion blew. He was also friends with most of the judicial employees and enjoyed visiting with them when time allowed. He contended that it was not *what* he knew but *who* he knew that made him effective.

The law office of Samuel Morton, Esq. was hardly ostentatious and consisted primarily of a modest private office, small conference room with an oversized oak rectangle table surrounded by ten old-fashioned oak chairs and a reception area which sported floor to ceiling built-in bookcases along the back wall. They were crowded with neatly placed law books and legal periodicals. An antique counter separated Jordan's work area from the comfortable chairs in the waiting area. Salty had rented a closet adjacent to his office in which he stored his files and supplies. Jordan was queen and ruled with an iron fist. Because the office was so small, she would not tolerate mess. Anything out of place affected the entire landscape not to mention her disposition. She was also fanatical about cleanliness. When she spoke, they jumped. To say she was obsessive/compulsive was an understatement. Easier to pick up your mess than fight with a she-devil the men often joked. All-in-all, the three of them were quite the happy little family.

As soon as he entered the office, Salty said: "Buddha, would you please run to the district attorney's office and obtain whatever discovery they have available. This early in the case I have little hope we would be provided with anything much more than the initial paperwork generated to hold Jas for arraignment but, who knows there might be more. We need to know what we're up against as soon as possible."

Buddha grabbed his motorcycle helmet and headed out the door. Although he owned a Range Rover, when the weather permitted he chose to ride his Harley to the office. Salty insisted he park his hog in the rear of the building so as not to hinder or annoy his more sophisticated clients who looked at the biker community with distaste. The ride to the DA's office was short. He was able to snake his way through traffic so the trip took less than thirty minutes. He returned with a copy of a warrantless arrest prepared by law enforcement to justify holding Jas in custody. The warrantless arrest form gave a thumbnail description of the crime barely enough to establish probable cause. Law enforcement only had to include enough details to convince a judge to sign the document to detain the accused pending a formal filing of charges. It stated Jas was found at the scene cradling the now deceased in her lap and covered with blood. It was weak at best but was sufficient enough for a judge to sign. There were scanty few police reports this early in the game. No surprise there! The preliminary reports revealed nothing that even remotely implicated Jas as the killer other than that she was at the scene. Working with what little information they had, Salty decided to request a preliminary hearing in order to get the prosecution to reveal the theory upon which they were basing their case. There had to be more than what was in the reports. Salty had Jordan prepare a demand for a preliminary hearing. He would file the document with the Court the following day.

The crime scene was still being processed so no forensic reports were yet available from that venue. The entire mansion was being fingerprinted. Fibers and other evidence were collected, marked and placed in plastic evidence bags. Telephone records and messages from the answering machines were examined. DNA samples were taken from the still unwashed dishes in the kitchen and other sources such as combs and toothbrushes from the bathrooms and outside photographs were taken of muddy tire tracks in the driveway due to the rain the day of the murder. Salty stood aside and observed since he was allowed only limited access to the crime scene. He concluded that law enforcement was doing a respectable job processing the scene. Viewing the scene in person at this early stage would be an advantage later at trial. Besides, no good defense lawyer would go to trial without having viewed the scene.

Means, motive and opportunity. Salty pondered the "big three" and wondered how Jas fit into the scheme in the eyes of the district attorney. Jas certainly had the means and opportunity, but how about motive? That was still a gnawing question. For now, all he could do was speculate. After all, his client was presumed innocent unless and until her guilt could be proven otherwise.

CHAPTER 9

WIND AND RAIN

The preliminary hearing was short and uneventful. The prosecution called only one witness to testify, Detective Sergeant Larry Bridges, the lead investigator. He testified that Jas was found at the scene just minutes after the murder. The time frame was determined by the victim still seeping blood and his body still warm. Reading from his notes, Bridges testified that according to the medical examiner's report, the victim could not have lived more than two or three minutes after the wound was inflicted because of the great loss of blood. The victim was pronounced dead at the scene. The report also stated that Jas was the only suspect who could have perpetrated the murder since no other person was found or observed in close proximity to the scene. The time frame was too tight and "Ms. Zachary" herself discounted the likelihood of alternate suspects by stating she had not seen anyone at the scene when she first arrived.

Salty objected to the hearsay statements (what Bridges was told and not what he personally observed). His objection was overruled as the rules of evidence, which Salty already knew, were relaxed at a preliminary hearing. Salty did not present any evidence and opted not to mention the Carlson vehicle leaving the estates because the time between when Jas saw the car and the time she found Nick would have to have been more than the two or three minutes the medical examiner noted in his report and would not be useful at this juncture and maybe not all.

At the end of the preliminary hearing, Judge Ralston found probable cause to bind the case over for trial. The parties then had to coordinate a date for trial along with deadlines for motions and/or other matters to be brought before the court. In the criminal justice system, the prosecution has a period of six months within which to conduct the trial unless the defense waived "speedy trial." Salty refused to waive speedy trial. He was convinced Jas was innocent or at the very least that there was no evidence to the contrary and he didn't want Jas to remain in jail longer than necessary since she was unable to make bond. She would have to post a cash, property or surety bond in the amount of $1,000,000. The very least she would be required to rise would be the $100,000 fee required of the surety (bondsman) representing one-tenth of the million dollar bond. She, of course, didn't have assets worth what was required so she would, in all likelihood, remain in jail until the conclusion of the trial. Jas was formally charged and advised on Monday, July 24 and entered her plea of not guilty. The six-month speedy trial period began when Jas entered a not guilty plea and was calculated to run through January 24. The trial would have to take place prior to January 24.

Judge Ralston frowned at his calendar, cleared his throat and asked the attorneys how long they anticipated trial would take. Salty said he would be filing motions, including a motion for change of venue. He, however, was not at all optimistic and anticipated that most of his motions would be denied. He also indicated he thought jury selection would take at least one week. Special Prosecutor, Sylvia Cooper, concurred. Cooper then informed the Court that the prosecution's case would take at least one week. Among the list of endorsed witnesses were three experts she anticipated she would be calling. Salty also asked for a week to present the defense case. Judge Ralston's only available three-week period was December 1 through December 21. All parties agreed to the December dates and so the trial of *The People of the State of New Mexico v. Jasmione Zachary* was set.

The motions hearing was scheduled for August 16. Salty filed motions for Change of Venue; Suppression of Physical Evidence; Suppression of Statements and Motion in Limine. All, as expected, were summarily denied.

Although success in trial hinges on the success of motions in most instances, Salty's resolve was not at all deterred. He was too much the professional to play Russian roulette and always had his ducks in a row no matter which way the ball bounced. He may have lost the battle but there was still a war to wage.

During the preparation of the case, Salty was haunted by Jas' statement that she saw the Carlson Realty car exit Nick's estate on several occasions. Jas told Salty she was familiar with the realty agency. She had seen Adell Carlson showing property in the area of and adjacent to her condo. The Carlsons were socialites and often had their pictures in the newspaper taken while attending various functions and Jas recognized Adell from those clippings. The explanation as to why Adell Carlson was at the estates so often and presumably at McGregor's residence remained a mystery and Salty pondered it and was perplexed in trying to fit the pieces together.

⦿⦿⦿⦿⦿

Knowing it was probably a long shot, Salty asked Buddha to interview Nick's neighbors and ascertain if any of them might have seen anything out of the ordinary or maybe seen the Carlson Realty Lexus at the crime scene on the afternoon of the murder.

There was nothing in the police reports indicating that law enforcement had interviewed any of McGregor's neighbors. The police apparently thought they "had their man" or more aptly "had their woman" and didn't deem it necessary to look any further. After all, Jas was at the scene. Her fingerprints were found on the murder weapon as well as various objects throughout the house. She was covered with the victim's blood. Her DNA was lifted from utensils in the kitchen and various items in the bathrooms. She was the only person present during the time frame it took McGregor to die. It was an open-and-shut case. It was just that simple. No need for the authorities to spend the time and expense hunting for an alternate suspect. Their energies were best spent "building" a case against Jas. She was the only one who could have done it.

Buddha was eager to do the interviewing. The next day he planned to scour the neighborhood in an effort to determine which neighbors were in the best position to view Nick's house most clearly. Since most of the terrain was desert and there were no large trees or high fences to block the view, Buddha decided he would interview the neighbors on all four sides as they all had, for all intents and purposes, an open view of Nick's home and driveway.

Buddha reported back to Salty that he planned to "surprise" the neighbors with his visit so they wouldn't have a chance to contrive a story or arrange not to be available. Salty agreed that was the best ploy. Salty said, "Buddha, I don't want you scaring young children and old women so could you trim that shaggy beard just a bit and look more like the brilliant investigator I know you to be. A different line of clothing would also help the total look; not that I have anything against worn, holey jeans and Harley Davidson T shirts but…."

Buddha replied, "Absolutely. However, I think your request transgresses into the realm of invasion of privacy and identity theft but for you, the world."

"Ahh, I bet you say that to all your employers."

"Yeah, especially the ones who pay me."

CHAPTER 10

SCATTERED SHOWERS

T he next day Buddha began his quest and started with the neighbor's house to the east of Nick's estate. The name on the mailbox declared the residents to be "The Sanders." Buddha rang the doorbell which resounded the first few bars of *The March of the Wooden Soldiers.* "How quaint," he muttered to himself. A woman in her mid-50s answered the door with what Buddha would later describe as an "irritated jerk."

"Mrs. Sanders?"

"Yes. Sorry, we do not allow solicitors…"

"I'm not selling anything. I'm investigating the murder of Nick McGregor. My I ask you a few questions?"

Relishing the thought of having attention directed towards her and being involved in a murder investigation, Mrs. Sanders replied, "My, yes. I was wondering when the police would get around to questioning me – come in."

"I'm not the police, I'm a private investigator," Buddha responded. "I was retained privately to try to fill in some gaps. Now, the day of the murder, did you notice anything unusual?"

"Well, no, nothing 'unusual.' The same old routine. One lady comes to visit and as soon as she leaves, another one shows up."

"Could you be more specific?"

"Of course. Several times a week a realty lady driving a silver Lexus arrives at Nick's in the early afternoon. I wondered if Nick was buying, selling or trading real estate as often as the visits occurred. Then when the realtor lady leaves, almost immediately that sweet little Jas shows up. She worked for Nick, you know, doing some redecorating. I visited with her at the mailboxes occasionally. I don't believe she could have killed him. She certainly could not have overpowered him and besides she didn't appear to be the type to do something like that."

"Did you see either the realty lady or Jas the afternoon Nick was murdered?"

"Yes, I saw them both. The realty lady had no more than left when Jas drove into Nick's driveway."

"Did you see anyone else besides the two women that afternoon?"

"No, I don't continuously stare out the window so there could have been other visitors that I wouldn't have noticed. But I did notice both the realty lady and Jas."

"Would you recognize the realty lady if you saw her again?"

"Of course. I saw her come and go several times a week for months."

"Can you describe her to me?"

"She's short and lumpy…"

"What do you mean 'lumpy'?"

"She has big breasts and an ample rear which, on such a short frame, makes her look lumpy.

Hummm, not too attractive either, dingy straight blond hair... I wondered what Nick saw in her. She just didn't seem his type. His deceased wife was 'movie star beautiful,' if you know what I mean."

"Yes, I've seen pictures of her and I do know what you mean. How long did the realty lady's visits usually last?"

"About an hour; sometimes more, sometimes less."

"And you're sure she was there the day of the murder?"

"Yes, I'm absolutely positive."

"Would you be willing to testify to that if need be?"

"Oh, my yes."

"Is there anything else you can add, anything at all?"

Mrs. Sanders looked thoughtful, then slowly shook her head and murmured "No."

Buddha said, "Thank you for your time. Here is my card. If you think of anything else even if you think it might not be useful, it may be, please call me."

137

"Oh, I will. Do you think I'll be called to testify?"

"At this stage, I can't say. However your willingness to do so goes a long way. We'll be in touch."

Buddha, having been encouraged by his first interview, proceeded to the neighbor on the west. The mailbox didn't announce who lived there so he had to wing it. He rang the doorbell. Much to his disappointment it was the boring quintessential doorbell ring. A mousy man, probably in his late 60s answered.

"Good afternoon, Sir. I'm Dave Jennings and I'm investigating the murder of Nick McGregor…"

BAM! The door slammed in his face. So much for feeling encouraged. Buddha thought, "Well, if at first, or second for that matter, you don't succeed, try, try again." And so he did. There were still two more directions to explore. Buddha drove to the house on the north which was far more elaborate than east or west. No doorbell here, just a black wrought iron door knocker attached to what looked like a lion's head. A maid, dressed in the traditional black dress/white apron uniform, albeit without the feather duster in her hand, opened the massive mahogany door. "Yes?" she said without smiling.

"Hello, my name is Dave Jennings. How are you today?"

"My name is Sophia and I'm well, thank you," she replied mockingly with an obvious foreign accent and a sudden twinkle in her eye.

"Sophia, that's a lovely name. Is it French?"

"Heavens, no! I was named after an Italian actress."

"But I detected a French accent when you spoke."

"If you did, you'd be the first – I grew up in Santa Fe. Do you have business with the Elmingtons?"

"Not necessarily. I'm investigating the McGregor murder and am canvassing the neighborhood to ascertain if anyone had seen anything suspicious on the day he was killed or knows anything about what may have occurred?"

"I've been expecting someone to question us ever since the murder took place. The Elmingtons are out for the day but I'd be happy to tell you what I know."

PAY DIRT! Thought Buddha as he asked "May I come in?"

"By all means but first please remove your shoes and leave them by the door."

Grudgingly, Buddha complied somewhat embarrassed by the hole in one sock that was glaringly apparent. Entering the mansion, he was awestruck by the elaborate motif and the enormity of the interior. Sophia, amused at his reaction, said, "Quit gawking and follow me to the kitchen." He was grateful she had not caught him gawking at her eye catching appointments.

Redirecting his gaze, Buddha cheerfully followed Sophia through the house to the kitchen in his stocking feet. Once he was seated at the marble counter with a glass of ice tea, Sophia asked in a chirpy voice, "So, what is it you want to know?"

"It's been rumored that a silver Lexus had been seen at Nick's house quite often and was there the afternoon he was murdered. I know you must keep very busy here but on the off-chance you might have…"

"Funny that you mention it," Sophia interrupted. "Of course, I noticed the comings and goings at Nick's.

I even started keeping a record of the women in-and-out because I suspected, having that many female visitors, it was just a matter of time before something happened."

Buddha thought he'd died and gone to heaven. He had found a witness who had kept score. He took a deep breath in an effort to quiet his excitement and said in as calm of a voice as he could muster: "Please go on."

"Two women were regulars. There were others occasionally but never regularly. That was before the pretty auburn haired woman appeared on the scene. I believe she is the one charged with his murder. He probably deserved it. I surmised he was a real womanizer. After auburn hair started visiting, all others ceased except for the real estate woman. She would show up early in the afternoon and leave just before auburn-hair drove up. She would drive out on cue as if she had received some kind of mysterious signal or order to get the hell out."

Buddha then asked, "How do you know all of this? Your line of vision from here appears to be pretty limited?"

With that, Sophia took his hand and led him up the massive spiral staircase. She took him to a bedroom at the front of the house overlooking the estates with a view of the entire neighborhood. Some front views; some back views. She pointed at the home directly across from the Elmington's mansion stating, "That's Nick's place." The view was of the back patio and the entire driveway. Buddha's heart stopped for one second. He drew in a quick breath and exhaled loudly. "So I see. Please continue."

"Since it was the weekend, the routine was different. Auburn hair would usually arrive earlier. That weekend, however, the Elmingtons had overnight guests for the annual tribal pow-wow summer festival in town so I was pretty busy. The front bedroom was being occupied by one of the guests and, as I tidied up the room, I glanced out but I didn't see anyone arrive or leave. I did notice Nick was bar-b-queuing steak on the back patio grill and seemed to be talking to someone inside. I couldn't make out who it was. It appeared to be a female figure just by the shape. After the cars traversed the driveway, they sometimes park out of my line of vision so I don't always see whose car is there.

Later in the evening we heard sirens and went outside to see what was happening. You know the rest, I assume."

Buddha stood nodding. This wasn't the eyewitness he had hoped for but.... He asked Sophia if he could have a copy of the journal she kept. She readily agreed to let him take it and copy it if he thought that would help. She first exacted his promise to promptly return it.

"Yes, it will be of enormous value in establishing that Nick had other visitors besides the one charged with his murder and a record of whom and when." Glancing through the journal, Buddha said, "Although you didn't know their names, recording the license numbers was a stroke of genius."

They went downstairs and Sophia walked him to the front door and opened it in a manner indicating, at least from Buddha's perspective, the interview was over. He thanked her for the ice tea and information. He slipped on his shoes and gave her his card asking her to call if she remembered anything else. He also told her he would return the journal to her as soon as possible and requested when it was returned that she

143

keep it in a safe place in case it would be required as evidence. She said she would and waved goodbye as he walked to his Range Rover.

Another direction and one last interview to conduct – the neighbors to the south.

South's mailbox was all duded up with dancing Kokopellis. The name painted in Southwest style on the mailbox was "The Shipleys." Buddha, buoyed by two positive interviews, walked briskly to the front door of the south mansion which was the lesser in stature of all the homes he had visited thus far. A "No Solicitors Allowed" sign was placed so it would not be hard to miss on the front portico. Buddha rang the doorbell and the door was opened by a small boy wearing thick pop-bottle type glasses.

"Can't you read?" the boy demanded.

"Hi, my name is Dave. Yes, I saw the sign but I'm not selling anything. Is your mother or father home?"

"Why?"

"I would like to speak to them."

"Why?"

Buddha put the palm of his hand to his forehead in exasperation and said, "It is grownup business. Let me please speak with your parents."

"Mom, some freaky looking guy wants to talk to you."

The boy's mother appeared, wiping her hands belligerently on her apron. "Yes, if you're selling," she said briskly, "we don't want any."

"Mrs. Shipley, forgive me for interrupting your cooking. I'm a private investigator," Buddha said handing her his card, "I'm interviewing Nick McGregor's neighbors to determine if any of you noticed anything unusual the day he was murdered."

Directing her attention at her offspring, she said sharply, "Malcolm, go watch your cartoons while I talk to this man." Then to Buddha she snapped, "How can I help?"

"Thank you for your time, Mrs. Shipley. Anything you observed would be useful. You have a fairly good view of the McGregor estate. I know how busy you must be with a child and big home to care for but perhaps you did notice…"

"You're absolutely correct! I am very busy, especially right now. We are having a dinner party and there's much to do. That damn catering service misplaced my order and now I have to do it all. Oh, never mind. I didn't see anything out of the ordinary and if I had, I would already have told the police. So, if you'll excuse me…"

"Yes, of course." Buddha knew when he was getting the bum's rush and decided not to pursue the conversation. "Thank you again for your time. You have my card if you…"

"Yes, yes. Good afternoon." Mrs. Shipley then slammed the door with so much force, Buddha jumped backward. He later told Salty he thought the action evinced "malicious intent."

CHAPTER 11

UNSEASONABLY WARM

As Buddha drove back to Salty's office, he was thinking of his 500 batting average. Not too shabby considering his team was in the cellar only hours before. Salty wasn't in the office when Buddha arrived. Jordan asked, "How'd it go?"

"We'll see what you think after I dictate my report. Two hits out of four tries is respectable. Will you type it for me?"

Jordan agreed. She typed in tandem with his dictation. When they got to the Elmington maid's interview, Jordan exclaimed, "Oh, my God, you hit a home run."

"Yeah, that's exactly what I thought."

"Do you have the journal?"

"Yep, right here."

Salty arrived back at the office in the middle of Buddha's dictation. Buddha interrupted to bring Salty up to speed and upon hearing the details of the morning's expedition, Salty was more encouraged, excited and enthused than he had been since he took on the case.

"Jordan, would you please prepare a Defendant's Additional Witness List listing all four of McGregor's neighbors."

"I'm already on it," she said, and handed him the completed document to sign.

"Wow, so efficient! That's why I pay you the big bucks."

This comment elicited eye rolling from Jordan and Buddha which Salty chose to ignore.

"I have to go back to court this afternoon so I'll file it then," Salty remarked as he bent to sign the document. Retreating towards his office he turned and said, "Good work, Buddha. Your interviews will certainly be a big help. By the way Jordan, how is it you're always a jump ahead of me?"

"Just lucky, I guess, besides I need to earn those 'big bucks'" Jordan answered and the three of them shared a hearty laugh which stemmed from years of comfortable familiarity.

❧

Even though the trial was months away, Salty began prepping for his opening and closing statements. He would jot down items as they occurred to him so that they didn't get lost in the maze. Means, motive and opportunity would be the crux of his defense – especially motive. What motive would Jas have had for killing Nick? This question still haunted him and perhaps always would.

At some point Salty would have to interview the neighbors in person and decide whose testimony would best benefit his client, maybe both. Of course, by listing all of the neighbors as witnesses, the prosecution would also have a crack at them. This did not trouble Salty if the two "good" witnesses were telling the truth and stuck to their story. He also felt the prosecution would get the same "warm" reception from the two uncooperative neighbors who had given Buddha the blistering brush-off.

Salty had spent many hours with Jas going over her story. He had never detected any deceit in her rendition. He resolved he would ask Cooper why the investigation didn't extend to Nick's adjoining neighbors. Was the prosecution that sure that Jas was the culprit and that they didn't need to look for alternate suspects? He would tell Cooper about the Carlson Realty involvement and see if he could exact a promise of further investigation. He also knew from the discovery documents that there were two separate sets of muddy tire tracks that had been photographed. There were multiple DNA samples that had been collected, as well as a variety of fingerprints. He would like to get a non-testimonial identification order from the court ordering the collection of DNA samples and fingerprints from Adell and her husband/partner, Winston Carlson. That might be tricky if the prosecution bowed its neck and objected to the issuing of the order. He would ask Cooper in advance if the prosecution had an objection to the process. Surely the prosecution was as anxious as he to bring the perpetrator to justice and not risk convicting an innocent person, namely Jas.

The next day Salty called the Albuquerque DA's office to make an appointment with Cooper. She told him she would be in Farmington on Monday and could meet with him then. She also stated that the prosecution did not object to the non-testimonial collection of samples from the Carlsons. Salty had Jordan prepare the appropriate document which he filed with the court. Judge Ralston signed the order and forwarded copies to law enforcement with instructions to collect samples of DNA and fingerprints from the Carlsons. Salty and Cooper also received signed copies of the order so they knew the process had been initiated and they could incorporate whatever the results revealed into their respective cases. They both knew normally it could take weeks to get the results, however, since this was a capital case, the lab would expedite the analysis and place this case close to the top, if not at the top of the list.

❦

After much consideration, Salty decided to play his trump card and have Buddha interview the Carlson woman. She would already be on notice from the issuing of the non-testimonial identification order. He knew it was a long shot and would probably alert her that she was being considered, if not by law enforcement then by someone, as a suspect.

Buddha, with pen and pad in hand, entered the Carlson Realty office. The office was spacious and elaborately styled with expensive furniture and artwork signifying an air of pomposity and prosperity. Buddha approached the reception desk and gave his business card to the mature but attractive receptionist identified as Renee Hanson by the name plate placed on the half-circle desk she sat behind. He asked to see Adell Carlson. Renee smiled up at him as she picked up the telephone and announced him. A minute later Adell

152

Carlson came out of her office and, thinking he was a client, extended her hand in greeting, asking him to "Please come in and have a seat."

Mrs. Sanders' description of a "short, dumpy woman with stringy dishwater blond hair" was dead on. He also noticed Sophia had nailed her as well but Sophia had been more than generous in labeling her "not too attractive." **BINGO!**

"Well, Mr. Jennings, how can we help you? What kind of property are you looking for?"

"Truthfully, I'm not looking for property. I'm here seeking answers to some lingering questions surrounding the McGregor murder." Buddha noticed Carlson's quick intake of breath, sudden change of facial expression and stiffening in her chair. What he did not know was that the two offices of the Carlson's were connected on an intercom system so that each could hear the other. As the two spoke, Winston Carlson was listening from his office with piqued curiosity.

"I'm not sure I know anything that would be of use," Adell said nervously, knowing Winston was listening.

"I have witnesses who will testify that they saw your car at the McGregor residence the afternoon of the murder. They will also testify your car was a regular at Nick's and that they observed you being there in the early afternoon on many occasions. Can you explain…"

"Well, I never! They're lying, of course. I was not there that day nor was I ever at his house."

Buddha, reminded of a former president denying an affair and saying words to that effect not too long ago, asked: "Did you have other business at the Desert Rose Estates?"

"Perhaps. Our business takes us all over San Juan County. I really couldn't say where I was the afternoon of the murder, except that I wasn't there."

Overhearing his wife's feeble denial, Winston's heart sank. He knew Adell was not faithful but he had always turned a blind eye. Now he was hit smack between the eyes with it and had to face the facts. "Oh, Adell," he thought, "oh, my dear, sweet darling." Quite obviously Winston was still very much in love with Adell despite her philandering. "Whatever would I do without you if you did this and were convicted?"

Buddha asked Adell if she was the only one who drove the silver Lexus.

"No, Winston also drives it on occasion."

This was when a plan began formulating in Winston's mind.

◦⊱⋆⊰◦

Although Adell was now not the beauty Winston first fell in love with, she was still his only love. She let herself slip after they were married. She put on weight and didn't take as much pride in her appearance as she had before. He found that he missed her physical beauty but he wouldn't trade her for *Venus*. Winston began reminiscing about when he and Adell first met. She was really something back then. She was lovely. Her figure was the envy of all the women and the fantasy of all the men. She was careful about her appearance. She had her hair styled weekly and her makeup was designed by a Hollywood cosmetologist. It suited her perfectly.

Adell captivated his heart although he was twenty years older than she. The two fell in love and married. Together they successfully built Carlson

Realty into a major money making machine. That is, until the crash hit in the mid-2000s. Even though the market slowed down, way down, the Carlsons were well protected because Adell was a financial genius and had a natural feel for the stock market. Even when times were hard she continued to invest wisely and make money.

Winston, now in his late seventies and not in the best of health, realized that his life-span was short and unpredictable. He was no longer able to enjoy sex, had to watch his diet, had so many aches and pains he couldn't even list them all and his lack of energy and the on-set of old-age in general kept him from doing things he had so thoroughly relished just a few years before such as golfing, boating and tennis. Even travelling was becoming tiresome. Adell, however, now in her fifties was still vibrant and enjoying life and why shouldn't she? She had given him so much pleasure during their time together he couldn't even conceive of life without her.

Winston suspected Adell did have something to do with the murder as he had done some recon work on his own and had spotted her car in McGregor's driveway on numerous occasions. He knew Adell to have a quick and sometimes violent temper. Musing over these things, Winston decided losing her would be a death sentence for him anyway. He decided at that moment that he would intervene if Adell was charged and brought to trial. He would confess to the murder and sacrifice himself to spare her if necessary. If he lost her he would have nothing left to live for anyway.

Buddha asked Adell if she knew Nick McGregor.

"Yes, I knew him. I remember him from my school days. Even though he had graduated years before I entered high school, he was still considered a Farmington High icon. He was quite the athlete and always featured in the local newspaper's sports page. The school trophy case is full of trophies that Nick had won or helped win for the Cougars. I understand he lived with his family in Albuquerque and worked for World Wide Airlines. His parents lived here and he visited often, or so the society section of the *Farmington Times* reported. His parents were very active in the Catholic Church and were featured in the paper from time-to-time, sometimes with pictures of

157

Nick and his family. After his parents were killed, Nick and his family moved back to Farmington to the family estate. That is pretty much all I really know about the McGregors and Nick in particular."

"How then do you explain your car being seen at Nick's so often?"

"I don't have to explain that because it never happened. How many times do I have to tell you that? Perhaps I should call my lawyer."

"That's up to you. I'm just trying to piece together some loose ends in an effort to arrive at the truth."

"I'm not answering any more of your ridiculous questions. This conversation is over. I'm politely asking you to leave."

At that moment, Winston barged into Adell's office. "Oh, excuse me, I didn't know you were busy. We have an appointment we're late for, Adell, and you know how very important this client is. Are you able to get away now?"

"Yes, you bet. We're done here. Good day, Mr. Jennings."

"Thank you for your time. I'll be in touch."

"I certainly hope not." Adell murmured under her breath.

Buddha left the realty office knowing that Adell was lying. He wanted to pursue the matter further but would have to confer with Salty and get permission to do some real detective work on his own.

Once Buddha was gone, Winston asked what the conversation had been all about.

In a huff, she said: "Oh, some busy bodies thought they saw my car at the Desert Rose Estates on the same day Nick McGregor was murdered. I categorically deny ever being there, much less on that day – now don't you start. I've had all I can take for one day. Besides, I assume you overheard our entire conversation."

Winston let the whole matter drop. His plan was in place and there was no use evoking Adell's ire. He was already relegated to the spare bedroom in the basement.

CHAPTER 12

BELOW FREEZING

D ecember 1 was a bitter cold, intensely windy day in Farmington. Despite the weather, the courtroom was packed to capacity. Salty thought from the public's interest in the trial and the expansive media coverage, if it came to it, he would appeal the change of venue denial and request a new trial in another city that wasn't quite as saturated with coverage. There were no guarantees the appeal would be granted but at least it could fall under the category of "Plan B". Since Nick and Jas were both lifelong residents of Farmington, public curiosity was much more intense than what it would have been otherwise. They both had a multitude of local friends. Jas owned and operated her own very successful business on Main Street and knew just about everyone in Farmington. She was on the boards of the Better Business Bureau and Chamber of Commerce. Nick was a retired World Wide pilot and a local celebrity of some stripe. Both were active in the Catholic Church as well as community organizations. Thus, the interest in this particular trial was overwhelming. It appeared there wasn't a soul in Farmington who hadn't heard of the "trial of the century" and the gallery was anxiously waiting for it to begin.

Jas, looking very thin and drawn, sat between Salty and Buddha at the defense table. The five months she spent incarcerated awaiting trial had taken its toll. She had no spare fat to begin with but managed to lose fifteen pounds anyway. Yvonne, who was constantly in touch with her as much as the jail allowed, bought Jas appropriate clothing for trial, and now wearing a black pants suit and white blouse, Jas seemed unaware that she was the center of attention. Her hair had lost

161

its luster and she was makeup-free except for some lip gloss which she applied to help ease her dry lips. Salty looking at her thought: *Despite everything she had been through, she was still appealing.* Something stirred inside him and he suddenly realized how much he was attracted to her – clearly beyond the bounds of the attorney/client relationship. *Could he be falling for her? No chance. But yet…*

Judge Ralston was heralded in by his clerk. All rose in response but were immediately instructed by the judge to remain seated. His Honor took the bench and pushed his glasses up with his right middle finger leaving one to ponder if the gesture had a more subtle symbolic meaning. Having perused the file on his desk, he then called to order the case of *People of the State of New Mexico v. Jasmine Zachary.* Judge Ralston peered over his glasses at the attorneys and asked if each was ready to proceed. He received two affirmatives.

The grueling task of selecting a jury commenced. It dragged on for almost a full week just as anticipated. Each prospective juror was basically asked the same questions or indiscernible variations thereof. To say it was boring to on-lookers was an understatement. However, to the participants, selecting the right jurors to sit in judgment was as paramount to winning the case as was the case itself. The defense and prosecution paid close attention to the answers to the various questions as well as the demeanor of the responding jurors. By noon on Friday, the fifth day of jury selection, the parties had agreed on the panel and the judge swore in the prospective jurors and seated them. Salty was neither hot nor cold on the group as a whole but liked several who he thought would weigh the evidence and return a "fair verdict." A "fair verdict," of course, was a verdict of not guilty. The panel consisted of seven women and five men of various ages and two alternates, both women. Salty was pleased there were more women than men for obvious reasons. He felt the women, for example, would be more sympathetic to Jas given the circumstances and Nick's social history.

By the time the ritual was completed it was 1:30 p.m. Judge Ralston recessed court until the following Monday. He charged the jurors not to read, listen to or view anything in the media or discuss or listen to discussions pertaining to the trial. He also charged the prosecution with being prepared to present its case. He had made it clear that no continuances or delays would be tolerated. Each side, he instructed, would be allowed only one hour to make an opening statement. Ralston was a strict enforcer of *his rules* and attorneys who appeared before him were often made painfully aware of his disdain for those who disregarded his mandates. Special Prosecutor Sylvia Cooper told the Judge the People would indeed be ready to proceed. She also informed both court and counsel that she would call her expert witnesses first, law enforcement personnel next and then the lay witnesses. Her presentation, she stated, would consist of nine witnesses.

⚜

Monday, January 14, was ushered in with the predicated heavy snowstorm which made traveling from place-to-place in Farmington difficult. Farmington's road department was still painfully pitiful and had not improved much since last year's Christmas storm. Nonetheless, the courtroom was packed with spectators. Salty, having to use the visitor's parking lot, was annoyed at how carelessly people had parked their cars because of their inability to see the lines dividing the parking spaces. He made a pass through the lot, but then decided to park on the street to avoid the hodge-podge environment created within the parking lot. The one and only snow plow had plowed the streets surrounding the courthouse in anticipation of heavy traffic due to the trial. Salty, arriving early was fortunate enough to get a parking spot on the street close to the front entrance. The city had placed bags over the parking meters proclaiming it was not necessary to pay on this day due to weather conditions. "Well," Salty thought, "things are looking up. Perhaps the rest of the day will be as amiable." Chuckling, he thought again, "At least, I still have my sense of humor." It was probably just as well he didn't know how long his sense of humor would last. Being the realist he was, however, he knew he would be severely tested.

Special Prosecutor Cooper was seated at the prosecution table rifling through a stack of files and their contents. Seated next to her was second chair, Deputy District Attorney Dan Williams. Cooper gingerly pulled a page from a file and placed it in front of her just as Salty approached. He said, "Good morning. I trust you had a pleasant weekend here in Farmington. We don't usually get this much snow. Did you order it?"

Cooper replied, "If I had that kind of pull, I'd be in a different line of work which would necessarily include reclining on a distant sunny beach somewhere warm and tropical." They all laughed good-naturedly and Salty crossed the aisle to set up shop at the defense table. After pulling out his work-product, he put his briefcase on the floor next to him. Buddha, who was already seated at the defense table, was dressed court appropriate and had his beard trimmed to a respectable length. When the door leading to the holding area opened, Salty and Buddha looked up just as Jas was being led in by a sheriff's deputy. She took her seat between Salty and Buddha. The sheriff's deputy retreated back to the holding area door and stood there alert and militarily erect. Since this was a high-profile case, more than the usual number of deputies were assigned courtroom duty and were strategically positioned throughout to maintain the peace and dignity of the court and as mandated by Judge Ralston.

Salty whispered to Jas, "I feel we have a good jury and our case is solid. We have a very good chance. Try to relax and not look so tense. Jurors notice every detail and their interpretation may not be accurate. Incidentally, you look very nice."

Jas smiled up at him and he squeezed her hand. Buddha touched her arm in a supportive gesture. The defense team was ready, more than ready, they were raring to go.

⊙⊛⊛⊛⊙

Judge Ralston looking up from the sheets of paper spread before him raised his eyebrows and asked, "Are the parties ready to proceed?"

"Yes, Your Honor," both the defense and prosecution answered virtually in unison.

"Very well, then, we will hear opening statements. You are each restricted to one hour. Ms. Cooper, you will go first!"

Rising and circling the prosecution's table, Cooper said, "Thank you, Your Honor. Good morning ladies and gentlemen, and thank you for venturing out on such a cold winter day to serve the people of San Juan County as jurors in the case before the court. We know the personal sacrifice you make by serving on a lengthy trial and we truly appreciate your willingness to do so.

"Opening statements are designed to acquaint the jury in broad strokes with what the parties intend to prove or disprove. They are the skeleton of the case, if you will, and will then be filled in with facts as the case proceeds through the trial process. We, the people, intend to prove to you beyond a reasonable doubt that the person charged, Jasmine Zachary, also known as Jas Zachary, is indeed the perpetrator of the murder of Nicholas McGregor. The evidence will show that no one else could have committed the act. The defendant was found cradling the victim at the scene of the crime soaked in his blood; her fingerprints were on the murder weapon; her DNA was found on the recently used unwashed dishes in the kitchen; her DNA was found on bathroom items such as combs and toothbrushes; her fingerprints were scattered throughout the house in various rooms; and, her bathing suit and

168

some personal items were also found in a guest bedroom in the mansion."

Cooper continued, "The evidence will show that the victim did not die instantly of what was determined to have been a stab wound. He bled to death because of that wound. Our expert witness, Forensic Pathologist Walter Grasso, will relate to you in his testimony the time frame within which it takes a man the size of the victim to bleed to death after suffering a wound similar to the one inflicted on the victim. The expert's estimate of the time frame is not long, two or three minutes. Furthermore, according to the defendant herself, she was the only person on the scene during the time estimated for the victim to die as stated in the forensic pathologist's report. If another person had committed the crime and made an escape before the defendant arrived on the scene, the victim would have surly been dead, albeit within a minute or so, before discovery of the body. The defendant stated she detected shallow breathing when she arrived and immediately called 911. Of course, the defendant is not a medical doctor but which one of us could not detect shallow breathing.

You, of course, don't have to have an MD behind your name to see a person's chest rise and fall."

Cooper circled the podium, pausing for effect before continuing. "There is a lengthy driveway leading to the victim's mansion. By the time the killer did the deed, exited the house and got to his or her car, a substantial number of those two or three minutes would have elapsed. Additionally, it is not likely that the two vehicles would have passed in the driveway, each undetected by the other if another person was leaving as the defendant arrived. The driveway is the only viable way in and the only viable way out."

Cooper went on and on regaling the jury with the people's case-in-chief well into the allotted hour. Most of her commentary was repeating what she had previously said with little variation and expounding on her experts' expected testimony. After what seemed like an eternity, she concluded by stating: "The people will erase any reasonable doubt you may have regarding the guilt of the defendant and, should the evidence warrant, we will be requesting that you return a guilty verdict at the conclusion of the trial. Thank you."

After Cooper took her seat, Judge Ralston said, "Mr. Morton, you may proceed with your opening statement at this time."

"Thank you, Your Honor. Ladies and gentlemen, I will be brief. I do not intend to put on my entire defense in my opening statement. I know you must be weary after having sat there for the last hour. I will briefly summarize the crux of our case." Salty then paused and deliberately rearranged, for the purpose of effect, some notes he had laid on the podium. Continuing, he said: "We will disprove, even though we are not required to do so, all of the people's claims that Ms. Zachary was the only person who could have committed the crime. Yes, she was there covered in the victim's blood but only because she was trying to save him. Her fingerprints were found on the murder weapon because she was trying to remove the knife in an effort to do all she could to help Mr. McGregor. Her DNA and fingerprints would naturally be found throughout the house because she spent a lot of time there working with Mr. McGregor on the remodel of his residence. She wasn't restricted to a few rooms. The remodel included every room in the mansion. She was invited by Mr. McGregor to enjoy the pool and cool off during the hot New Mexico afternoons so her swimsuit and other personal items would obviously be present. As far as Ms. Zachary noticing 'shallow breathing,' that can be attributed to her state of mind in wanting him to be alive. It could also be attributed to her cradling him thus forcing air out of his dead lungs. Who knows how many scenarios could apply. How does all of this add up to her having committed the crime?"

Salty took a deep breath and paused to let his last statement sink in. He stood erect at the podium and proceeded with his opening: "The medical examiner's time frame is only an estimate or what one might call an 'educated guess.' It could be wrong. By adding a few minutes, another person could have been present, committed the murder and fled before the defendant even turned into the driveway. My client will testify, even though she is not required to do so, that she passed another car in the estates before she got to the McGregor driveway. There were two sets of muddy tire prints in the driveway to substantiate her testimony. Where did the second set come from if there hadn't been another vehicle present immediately after the

172

afternoon rain? And, for that matter, it's possible the perpetrator could have been on foot. The defense will prove to you that there is a reasonable doubt, more than a reasonable doubt, that the defendant committed the crime with which she is charged. More important than the aforementioned evidence, is the fact that the defendant had no motive for killing Mr. McGregor. We have a standard that we use in the legal profession – means, motive and opportunity. These are the three elements needed to sustain a conviction. Yes, she had the means and the opportunity but one does not usually just go about killing people without a motive. The prosecution did not suggest a shred of evidence that the defendant had a motive for killing Mr. McGregor. She worked *for* him. Why would she want to eliminate an additional source of income? It just doesn't make sense. And, if she were guilty why wouldn't she have fled from the scene? The evidence will show that she not only stayed at the scene, but called 911 and feverishly tried to revive Mr. McGregor. Is that what a guilty person would do? Or, did Ms. Zachary do what an innocent person would have done?

"I'm positive that after all the evidence has been presented and all the witnesses have testified you, too, will be convinced my client is innocent. Your service as jurors is greatly appreciated and I know you will do the right thing at the conclusion of trial and find Jasmine Zachary not guilty of all the charges brought against her. Thank you."

Judge Ralston mused as Salty sat down, "No wonder he is feared by his advisories and known for the ferocious defense of his clients. I'm already wondering about the defendant's guilt and I haven't even heard any evidence." He then announced, "We will break for lunch and reconvene at 2:00 p.m. sharp to start testimony."

The courtroom rapidly emptied as the gallery was anxious for the lunch break after sitting for such a long period of time. The bailiff took the jury back to the jury room where lunch was catered in. Jas was escorted back to the holding area and provided lunch which she hardly touched. Her emotions were running wild and her stomach in a knot. She was relieved that at long last the trial was underway as the waiting was torture but, on the other hand, she was scared stiff at what the outcome might be. Jas was somewhat encouraged after hearing Sam's opening statement. Even knowing she was guilty of the crime, she was able to see the logic the jury could glean from his rendition of what could and in all probability would cause reasonable doubt. At least the DA hadn't requested the death penalty should the jury render a guilty verdict. Even at that she didn't know if she wanted to go on living incarcerated for the rest of her life should the jury return a guilty verdict. The death penalty might be a blessing should that occur.

Salty and Buddha crossed the street to the deli and ordered to-go. Salty wanted to review his notes before testimony officially commenced so they retired to an interview room at the courthouse to eat while they worked. When Salty was in trial his mind was focused on the task at hand and he engaged in little else to the extent of shutting out even the conversations that went on around him. Buddha knew not to interrupt when Salty was concentrating so he went to the window to eat his sandwich and watch the snowflakes falling aimlessly to the ground.

After the lunch break, Judge Ralston took the bench and without further ado rapped his gavel and barked: "Call your first witness, Ms. Cooper."

The bailiff had the witness list and order in which the witnesses would be called. She went to the main door of the courtroom and summoned Dr. Walter Grasso, the first witness on the list.

Dr. Walter Grasso entered the courtroom with a swagger which implied a great deal of self-confidence or more appropriately egotism. He walked up to the reporter's table and raised his right hand without being told to do so. Quite obviously he was no stranger to the courtroom and wanted the jury to know it.

Judge Ralston did his own swearing in and asked Grasso, "Do you solemnly swear to tell the truth, the whole truth and nothing but the truth so help you God?" Judge Ralston did not agree with the decree to eliminate "God" from the oath and he refused to do so. If the witness didn't believe in God then it was a moot point. However, if the witness was a believer having to swear to God may have some effect on the truthfulness of the testimony about to be rendered. If a witness even thought about challenging the oath, one look at the expression on the judge's face would be dissuasion enough.

"I do," responded Dr. Grasso.

The judge gestured to Dr. Grasso to be seated and, directing his attention at the prosecutor's table, said: Ms. Cooper…"

"Thank you, Your Honor. Doctor, would you please state and spell your full name, your address and occupation for the record?" Cooper said as she walked to the podium.

"My name is Walter Paul Grasso, W A L T E R P A U L G R A S S O. I live at 24627 Bernalillo Avenue, Albuquerque, New Mexico. I work for the New Mexico Bureau of Investigation, NMBI, located in Albuquerque. I have been so employed for eighteen years."

"Thank you, Dr. Grasso. What is your exact field of expertise?"

"I am a forensic pathologist."

"Would you, for the jury, please explain in layman's terms what a forensic pathologist does?"

"I examine bodies to determine cause of death."

"Thank you, Doctor. Your Honor, the defense was provided with Dr. Grasso's curriculum vitae through discovery. Does the defense desire us to go through his education, training and experience or will the defense stipulate to Dr. Grasso's qualifications?"

Judge Ralston asked, "Mr. Morton?"

"In the interest of conserving judicial time, Your Honor, the defense will stipulate to Dr. Grasso's qualifications."

"So noted on the record. Ms. Cooper, you may proceed."

"Dr. Grasso, would you please take us through the autopsy of Nicholas McGregor and explain what your findings revealed?"

"Yes. I conducted an autopsy on Nicholas McGregor on July 25 at Sacred Heart Hospital here in Farmington. My examination disclosed that Mr. McGregor died of a knife wound to the chest just below the heart. The weapon was a smooth blade knife, six inches long with a four inch handle. The initial wound was not sufficient enough to instantly kill the victim. He died from bleeding out over a period of time. I would estimate no more than two or three minutes.

"In your opinion, Dr. Grasso, would a woman be able to administer a wound of that nature?"

"Oh, yes. The knife penetrated the soft tissue between the ribs just under the heart."

"Thank you, doctor. I have no further questions."

"Mr. Morton, your witness," said Judge Ralston.

"Dr. Grasso, did you observe any other marks, either fresh or healed, on Mr. McGregor's body?"

"No. As far as I could determine, he was in perfect physical condition except, of course, for the knife wound."

"And you state that a woman would be able to administer that serious of a wound. Was the victim stabbed from the front or back?"

"He was stabbed from the front."

"In your opinion, Doctor, would the victim have seen the assault coming? In other words, would the perpetrator have had to thrust the knife forward rather than just slip it into the victim's body?"

"Hummm, I would say a thrust was in order given the excellent physical condition of the victim.

His muscle tone would have made it somewhat difficult to just slip the knife in."

"So, being assaulted from the front, the victim most likely saw the blow coming and would probably have fended it off. And if that were the case, wouldn't he have other defensive wounds on his body?"

"Well, yes, but this is only speculation."

"My point is, Doctor, a woman the size of my client would find it difficult to subdue the victim while she stabbed him if he was inclined to fend off the assault. He would then most likely have other defensive wounds probably on his hands or arms. Would you agree with that?"

"Yes, I would agree. However, we don't know if the victim saw it coming and therefore would have had time to fend it off. All we know for certain is that he was stabbed from the front and eventually bled out from the wound."

"Thank you, Doctor. I have no further questions Your Honor."

"The witness may step down." The judge waited for Dr. Grasso to clear the witness box and exit the courtroom. He then said, "Ms. Cooper, you may call your next witness."

Cooper nodded to the bailiff who then called Marcus Salazar, the next name on the prosecution's witness list. After the witness was sworn in by Ralston, Cooper asked him to state and spell his name and give his address for the record. She again asked the defense to stipulate to the witness' curriculum vitae. Salty said the defense would so stipulate.

Cooper began, "Mr. Salazar, what is your field of expertise."

"I am a fingerprint expert, I compare and analyze fingerprints. I am employed by the New Mexico Bureau of Investigation and have been so employed for nine years."

"Did you find prints on the murder weapon recovered from Nicholas McGregor's body?"

"Yes, the only prints on the murder weapon matched back to those of the defendant, Jasmine Zachary."

"Would you be able to tell if any other prints on the knife had been wiped away or smeared prior to Ms. Zachary handling it?"

181

"No, there is no way to establish that especially with the amount of blood that had accumulated on the handle."

"What other prints were present at the crime scene?"

"Most of the fingerprints I examined belonged to Nicholas McGregor, Ms. Zachary and an Adell Carlson. There were numerous other prints throughout the mansion but none matched any known samples we had on file."

"And for further clarification, you testified there were 'numerous' fingerprints throughout the mansion but only three sets were identifiable, those of Ms. Zachary, the victim and Adell Carlson, is that correct?"

"Yes, that is correct."

"Thank you, Mr. Salazar. The people have no further questions."

"Your witness," the judge said to Salty.

"Mr. Salazar, you stated the only identifiable prints belonged to the victim, Ms. Zachary and Ms. Carlson. How many other sets of prints were collected from the scene?"

"Oh, numerous sets - I would say fifteen or so."

"Did you attempt to match those prints with any you had on file at the NMBI?"

"Yes, we examined every set that we collected. There were no matches in *our* records. But, then our records aren't complete."

"No matches in *your* records. What other records were available?"

"We don't have the luxury of sending our evidence to DC to be run on the main system containing millions of fingerprints. So to answer your question, no other records were available to us."

"Mr. Salazar, given the seriousness of the charges, wouldn't you think a complete and thorough examination was warranted?"

"Yes, sir, I do. However, we only have X-amount of resources and we do the best we can with what we have and what is made available to us."

"Thank you, Mr. Salazar, no further questions."

"Your Honor, I have a redirect for the witness," said Cooper.

"Go ahead, Ms. Cooper."

"Were these prints handled in the same way all other prints would be handled. Specifically, did you examine the prints collected from the McGregor mansion the same way you would examine any other prints brought to your office for identification?"

"Yes. I do not cut corners or do sloppy work. I take pride in my work and always endeavor to do the best job I can with what we have."

"Thank you. No further questions."

The last expert witness, Leonard Johnston, was called and asked to give the same identifying information. Upon completion of the routine, Cooper asked, "Mr. Johnston, what is your field of expertise?"

"I am a chemist. I examine samples of DNA and other bodily fluids as well as any other evidence collected from crime scenes. I have worked for the NMBI one month short of twenty-two years."

"Mr. Johnston, will you describe for the court and jury what evidence you examined that was collected from the McGregor crime scene and what your findings were?"

"Yes. Upon examination, the murder weapon revealed that the only blood on the knife belonged to the deceased."

"Is this the same knife you examined for blood samples?" Cooper asked handing a knife in a plastic evidence bag to the witness.

"Yes, it is. The knife we examined had a notch toward the end of the wooden handle and I can clearly see it there on the handle and I can attest that this is one and the same."

"Thank you. Please continue with your testimony as to the rest of the evidence examined from the crime scene.

"Well, I had a multitude of dishes, glasses and utensils from the kitchen that I examined. I found an abundant amount of the deceased's DNA as well as that of Ms. Zachary's on these items. I also found a small amount of DNA on a drinking glass corresponding to a sample of saliva taken from Adell Carlson which was obtained pursuant to a non-testimonial identification order issued by the court. Other samples taken were not identifiable. Items taken from the bathrooms were likewise linked back to the deceased and Ms. Zachary. Nothing in the bathrooms matched Adell Carlson's known DNA sample. I also examined the photographs of the tire tracks. They matched Ms. Zachary's car and also a car belonging to Carlson Realty. These tracks were photographed the day of the murder as it had rained and the tracks were still very clear."

"Thank you, Mr. Johnston. I believe you covered your examinations very thoroughly. I have no further questions."

"Your witness, Mr. Morton," said Judge Ralston.

Salty rose and walked boldly to the podium. "Mr. Johnston, you testified you were able to match three samples of DNA to three known persons, Ms. Zachary, the victim and one Adell Carlson. However, there was other DNA tested that you could not match because you had no known source, is that correct?"

"Yes, that is correct."

"And, you stated there were two separate sets of tire tracks photographed the day Mr. McGregor was murdered. Law enforcement was able to obtain photographs of the tracks only because it had rained earlier that day. Otherwise, it would have been impossible to determine how many vehicles may have visited the residence on that particular day. Is that correct?"

"Yes."

"So, to summarize your testimony, Mr. Johnston, what I ascertain is that although you were able to match evidence to known samples you had in hand, there was a plethora of evidence collected that could not be matched. Do you concur with that summary?"

"Yes, that sounds about right."

"Then how is it my client, Ms. Zachary, has been singled out as the perpetrator of the crime when it is obvious there were others at the scene who are faceless and nameless? She was found covered with the victim's blood trying to comfort him; she attempted to remove the knife from his chest hoping that would improve his chance of survival; she did not attempt to wipe her prints from the murder weapon; she did not try to cover up any evidence or leave the scene, in fact, she was the one who called 911 and summoned help immediately upon discovering the body. Does that sound like something a murderer would do? Or could one of the unidentified have committed the murder?"

"OBJECTION!" shouted Cooper, as she erupted from her seat. Johnston, however, had begun to answer: "I'm not qualified to answer that question…"

Judge Ralston somewhat agitated, said: "Mr. Morton, save some of your opinions for your closing argument. Objection sustained. The jury is instructed to disregard the question and answer. The witness is instructed not to respond until I have ruled on an objection." Johnston quickly apologized. Now it was Salty's turn.

"Yes, of course, I apologize. I was just incensed that the evidence you and the other experts tested was construed to make my client look like the only one who could possibly have committed the murder when there are others who are also likely suspects. My client had no motive to kill Nick McGregor, her only involvement with him was employment. Everything she did upon discovering the body indicates she wanted to save his life, not end it. Is that not true?"

"YOUR HONOR, OBJECTION! The defense is going beyond the scope of direct."

"Objection sustained, Mr. Morton…."

"Yes, Your Honor. I believe I've completed my cross. Thank you, Mr. Johnston."

It was 4:30 p.m. by the time the prosecution's experts finished testifying. Judge Ralston, after instructing the jury not to read, listen to or discuss anything about the case at bar, announced court would adjourn for the day and would reconvene at 9:00 a.m. the following morning.

And at 9:00 a.m. sharp the following day, Judge Ralston called the court to order.

Salty marveled at the way Judge Ralston conducted his courtroom. He was definitely a no-nonsense judge and was earning the respect of the defense team.

Cooper began by calling her law enforcement witnesses. The law enforcement and emergency team witnesses testified as to what they observed upon arrival at the scene. According to them, Defendant Zachary was sitting on the floor in a puddle of blood cradling the victim and sobbing uncontrollably. Her only statement was that she found him like that and called 911.

The investigators testified as to the manner in which they collected and handled the evidence at the crime scene and how they transported the evidence to the New Mexico Bureau of Investigation in Albuquerque. They stated they personally handed each of the experts the sealed bagged evidence and had the experts sign a receipt for the same. This was the protocol in place to preserve what was called in police parlance the chain of custody. There was nothing new or unexpected presented by law enforcement or the EMTs presentation. Their testimony was bland and was considered *pro forma*.

Salty cross-examined each witness and, satisfied that they were all telling the truth, did not try to impeach them.

Cooper informed the court that the prosecution's case was complete and that the People rested. So, at 4:45 p.m. Judge Ralston announced they would recess for the day and commence again at 9:00 a.m. the following morning when the defense would be called upon to present its case. The jury was escorted out. Jas was returned to jail and soon the courtroom was empty. Salty and Buddha, upon leaving the courthouse were greeted by ten inches of white fluffy snow that had fallen during the afternoon court session. As the two of them parted, they arranged to meet at Salty's office at 6:00 a.m. the following morning to continue preparing the defense's case-in-chief. Salty was buoyed by how the day had gone and waited in excited anticipation for his turn "in the barrel." After hearing the experts' testimony, Salty decided to alter his strategy with regard to the phraseology of some of his questions in order to adjust to the tempo established by the prosecution's case-in-chief.

CHAPTER 13

FLASH FLOODING

Promptly at 9:00 a.m. the following morning, court reconvened. Judge Ralston, in his morning voice, said, "Mr. Morton, you may call your first witness."

"The defense calls Adell Carlson," Salty announced. As with the prosecution witnesses, the bailiff had the defense's list of witnesses indicating the order in which they would be called.

Salty knew Adell would be a hostile witness from Buddha's interview of her. He didn't know exactly what to expect which was a deviation from tradition and a breach of the cardinal rule "Don't ask the question if you don't know the answer." He felt Adell was most likely the murderer and decided to chance it and call her to the stand anyway. He was fairly sure that the benefits of her testimony would outweigh the detriments and might very well be the lynch-pin in the defense's quest for an acquittal.

The bailiff exited the courtroom and summoned Adell who was waiting in the corridor with Winston and the other sequestered witnesses. Adell and Winston were quietly holding hands waiting in nervous anticipation. When Adell's name was called, they both jumped. Adell looked at Winston with a worried expression, squeezed his hand and walked briskly toward the courtroom. As she entered, she tentatively looked around. The gallery was looking back at her. Adell was dressed prim-and-proper in a dark suit. Her white high necked blouse was buttoned to the top. Judge Ralston beckoned her to the front of the courtroom and swore her in. As she took the witness stand she, understandably, looked apprehensive and sat in a stilted pose with her hands clasped together in her lap.

Salty let the drama mount as he slowly rose and moved to the podium. He stood there a minute shuffling through the notes on his tablet. He paused and looked up at Adell and looked down at his notes once more.

The judge shifted impatiently in his chair and frowned down at Salty. "Mr. Morton," he said in an irritated voice, "we're waiting."

"Of course, Your Honor. Just one moment. I seem to have misplaced something... oh, here it is." Then, directing his gaze at the witness, Salty asked, "Would you please state your full name and spell it for the record?"

"Adell Jean Carlson, A D E L L J E A N C A R L S O N."

"And, Mrs. Carlson, are you employed?"

"Yes, I am. My husband, Winston, and I own our own business."

"And what type business might that be?"

"We own and operate Carlson Realty."

"Is your business located in the city of Farmington?"

"Yes, of course."

"Do your day-to-day operations take you beyond Farmington proper?"

"Why, yes. We do most of our showings in town but we also operate throughout all of San Juan County as well. We are licensed to sell anywhere in New Mexico but, since we are fairly isolated here as far as being close to other populated New Mexico towns, we, for the most part, stay fairly close to home."

"Are you familiar with The Desert Rose Estates?"

"Most certainly. That was and is a major project. The contractors have been working on expanding it and are still building there. There are some stately old mansions peppered in with the new construction. It has become somewhat of a showplace and the old and new complement each other creating a charming atmosphere conducive to successful sales."

Adell answered the question sounding every bit like a real estate agent talking to a client.

"Do you spend much time in that area?"

195

"I don't know what 'much time' means. Would you clarify?"

"Are you there quite often in the early afternoons on week days?"

"Quite often? No."

"Let me remind you that you're under oath. Do you understand the consequences of perjury? You could be charged and convicted of a felony which would mean forfeiting your real estate license. Now, with that in mind, do you desire to change your answer to the last question?"

Adell fidgeted in her chair, crossed and uncrossed her legs, seemed unable to find a comfortable position for her arms and finally said, "Yes, I would like to restate my last answer. I do visit The Desert Rose Estates regularly and frequently visited an old friend who once lived there."

"And, what is your old friend's name?"

Adell, knowing there was no escaping giving the answer simply said, "Nick McGregor."

The courtroom became hushed. You could hear a pin drop. It seemed the gallery was holding its collective breath for more than a healthy length of time.

"Mrs. Carlson," Salty continued, "would you say perhaps every weekday you paid Mr. McGregor a visit?"

"Maybe. I don't know if it was *EVERY* weekday but quite often nonetheless."

"What were you doing at Mr. McGregor's house every day?"

After a long pause, Adell muttered what sounded like: "I refuse to answer that question!"

At least Judge Ralston interpreted it that way. In a stern voice, he barked: "Mrs. Carlson, you cannot withhold pertinent information concerning this case! I'm ordering you to answer the question!"

"No, I will not answer the question," Adell said defiantly.

"I will give you one more chance to answer. Otherwise, I am going to hold you in contempt of court. Mrs. Carlson, answer the question!"

Adell just sat there and glared at the judge. After a long pause, Judge Ralston ordered, "Guard, take Mrs. Carlson into custody." And, looking at Adell, the judge said with controlled anger, "I'm holding you in contempt of court."

197

A deputy sheriff handcuffed and escorted Adell out the side door of the courtroom but Winston, waiting for his turn to testify, was in a position to observe that Adell was handcuffed and had been placed in custody. His first thought was that she had been arrested for Nick McGregor's murder. He then decided to throw himself on his sword.

Judge Ralston declared a ten-minute recess and "invited" the attorneys to join him in his chambers.

"Morton, I'm giving you fair warning. You will not turn my courtroom into a circus. Do you have any more theatrics up your sleeve?"

"Your Honor, I did not plan or even imagine my witness would react in such a fashion. In fact, she was in essence not my witness but a 'hostile witness.' My next witness is her husband, Winston Carlson, a hostile witness as well, and I cannot guarantee he will not react much the same way."

The judge grunted but was unable to do anything about the situation. He had never been overturned on appeal and did not intend to start this late

198

in his career. He understood only too well the uncertainties of trial and the precarious nature of hostile witnesses.

When court reconvened, Salty asked the bailiff to call Winston Carlson. Winston, encouraged by his determination, walked briskly to the front of the courtroom, was sworn in and took the witness chair.

"Would you please state and spell your name for the record?" Salty began.

Winston was anxious to get it over with as quickly as possible. He answered, "My name is Winston Carlson, W I N S T O N C A R L S O N. I want to confess to murdering Nick McGregor."

There was a gasp and the courtroom erupted into a wild frenzy. Judge Ralston pounded his gavel with so much force that it broke under the strain. Jas became faint. Salty stood paralyzed, unable to fathom what he had just heard. Buddha looked from Jas to Salty unsure of what to do. To say chaos ruled supreme would be an understatement.

When the judge finally restored order and, masking anger fairly well, asked Salty to continue in his examination of Winston Carlson.

Not wanting this opportunity to slip through his fingers, Salty asked Winston for details.

Winston replied: "I will not make a statement other than I killed Nick McGregor. That's all I'm going to say."

Salty, still recovering from the shock, made a motion to dismiss the case against Jas on the grounds that Winston's confession of having murdered Nick McGregor was tantamount to an exoneration of his client.

The judge looked at Cooper with raised eyebrows. "Well…," he said.

A stunned Cooper asked the Court if she could briefly examine the witness and was granted the request.

"Mr. Carlson, when you admitted to killing Nick McGregor, did you realize that this was a capital offense punishable by either life in prison or death? Knowing this, do you still persist in your claim that you perpetrated the murder?"

"Yes, I do understand the consequences of my actions. I don't want innocent people like Ms. Zachary to be punished for something I did."

Cooper paused and Salty asked, "Your Honor, may I ask the witness a question?"

"Proceed."

"Mr. Carlson, was Jasmine Zachary, the defendant in this case, in any way involved in Nick McGregor's death?"

"Absolutely not!" was the firm response from Winston.

Never having been faced with such a dilemma, Judge Ralston recessed court until the following day. To the jurors, he reiterated his previous dictate only this time with more authority. Do not, and I repeat, do not listen to, read or watch anything that might appear on television or any other news source concerning this trial. Do not talk about the case among yourselves. You will report back here at 9:00 a.m. tomorrow morning." Then he ordered the attorneys to meet with him in chambers.

The courtroom was cleared. Jas, having been revived, was returned to her cell. Winston was taken into temporary custody to be interrogated by law enforcement concerning his confession. The attorneys left to meet with the judge in his chambers and Buddha said to no one in particular, "I thought those Perry Mason trials were somewhat farfetched when a witness, suddenly confronted with incriminating evidence, confessed to the crime on the stand. I guess Salty 'one-upped' Perry. He didn't even have to present evidence to get his witness to confess."

Sitting on her cold hard bunk, alone in her cell, Jas wallowed in confusion.

My head is spinning. What on Earth just happened? Why in the world would Winston Carlson confess to something I did? I just don't understand what's going on. Surely this isn't God's doing. If it is, I don't deserve it. Is this all still part of a bad dream?

CHAPTER 14

CLEAR SKIES

Judge Ralston sat behind his modest desk in a not so modest leather swivel chair. He was beginning to look haggard and perplexed. He finally said to Cooper and Salty, "Where do we go from here?"

Salty, having had a few minutes to compose his thoughts, decided he would ask for dismissal with prejudice which would prohibit Jas from ever being retried for the murder of Nick McGregor under any circumstances. Salty looked at Cooper and articulated his proposal. Cooper began shaking her head, "I don't know," she said, "The evidence certainly points to your client as the perp."

"And how does that outweigh an outright confession?" Salty retorted. "It's obvious you are prosecuting an innocent defendant."

"You have a point. In the interest of justice, the People will concur with the defense's proposal and dismiss the case, only without prejudice."

"Unhuh! No dice. Dismissal with prejudice or we finish the trial."

"Ms. Cooper," Judge Ralston interjected, "do you see any other outcome if the case is decided by the jury? They heard Carlson confess on the stand. My feeling is if you pursue this case to the end you will certainly alienate the jury and may I remind you this is a jury that has already sat through over two weeks of trial. Besides, a conviction under the circumstances would be a recipe for reversal. Do you really think the jury will now return a guilty verdict?"

"You make a good point, Judge. One wouldn't want to alienate the jury, now would one? On a more serious note, I really do not see any other alternative. If the jury returned a not guilty verdict that would be the same as dismissal with prejudice. So, in order to save judicial time and spare the defendant more anxiety than necessary since it appears she did not commit the murder, I will not oppose the defense's request."

"Fine. Mr. Morton, will you prepare the appropriate motion and order and have them ready when we reconvene tomorrow morning? Needless to say, I will be granting the motion."

"Your Honor, it would be my pleasure indeed. Thank you both. If there's nothing else, I would like to go see my client and tell her the good news."

"Yes, of course. I have nothing else. Ms. Cooper?"

"No, Your Honor. The prosecution has nothing further."

CRAFTED

Jas sat nervously twisting a tissue. When she heard the outer door of the pod open she jumped to her feet. Moments later Salty was being ushered into her cell. She threw her arms around his neck and hugged him. He gently pushed her back and looked into her innocent big blue eyes. "I have some good, no, great news," he began. "The court will be dismissing your case with prejudice when we reconvene tomorrow morning."

The case is going to be dismissed and WITH PREJUDICE. Can it be?

Jas knew from her brief summer job working for lawyers that "with prejudice" meant she could never be retried for the same crime. If it was dismissed "without prejudice" and more evidence or other circumstances surfaced, she could be brought back and retried. In legal terms, once the case was dismissed *with* prejudice or the jury found the defendant not guilty, jeopardy attached and to bring the defendant back before the court on the same charges would be considered "*double jeopardy*" and not constitutionally permitted.

Oh, please God, don't let anything happen between now and tomorrow to unravel the dismissal agreement. I really didn't mean to kill Nick and I'm ever so sorry. I miss him so much I can hardly bear it. Please forgive me.

206

Although the skies were cloudy and gray and snow loomed in the forecast, the defense team was elated when they returned to court the following morning. Jordan accompanied Salty and Buddha as this was a "red-letter" day. Jordan sat in the gallery directly behind the defense table. When all parties were present and the courtroom was filled to capacity with lookie-loos, the judge entered and beckoned to the bailiff to call the court to order. Without ceremony, Judge Ralston asked Salty if he had a motion to present.

"Yes, Your Honor, I have a Motion to Dismiss With Prejudice and a proposed Order."

"Ms. Cooper, do you have any objection to the granting of said motion?" Judge Ralston asked.

"No, Your Honor, the People concede and offer no objection."

Once again the courtroom became chaotic. Reporters trampled over spectators and each other to get to the telephones in the corridor. Judge Ralston broke another gavel in a futile attempt to restore order. When the frenzy finally subsided, Salty asked to approach the bench and was granted permission. He presented the judge with the Motion to Dismiss and

Judge Ralston signed the Order granting the same with a flourish. The prosecution had previously been given a copy of the motion for their approval and it bore Cooper's signature. After signing the order, the judge gave the bailiff the signed original to make copies for all parties.

"This case is hereby dismissed with prejudice," Judge Ralston announced in a subdued tone. "Ms. Zachary, this means you are free to go." He then rose and gingerly left the courtroom which was still buzzing with the excitement over the revelation of the dismissal. Only now, the dismissal was official and Jas would be set free.

The bailiff reappeared and distributed conformed copies of the signed order to each of the attorneys. Jas lovingly fingered Salty's copy. She looked up at him with tears in her eyes. He took her in his arms and they hugged each other, lingering longer than necessary conveying even to the uninitiated more than just gratitude. After embracing Jas, Salty and Cooper met mid-way between their respective tables and shook hands in a gesture of mutual respect. Cooper had her briefcase packed and, as she headed toward the door, she turned and said to Salty, "If I ever get in trouble, you're the man! How'd you pull that off?" They both knew she was kidding – sort of.

The defense team waited at the jail and upon Jas' release they headed back to Salty's office with Jas in tow. Jordan had bought and had on ice some champagne to celebrate. Even though it was barely noon, champagne was passed around and the four of them raised their glasses high in grateful homage to the powers that be. After they had exhausted the bottle, Salty invited all to lunch and the celebration continued into the late afternoon.

When the party finally waned, Jas told Salty she wanted to return to the jail and pick up her belongings. Salty drove her to the jail and went in with her to retrieve the personal items that had been confiscated at the time of her booking. The evidence custodian handed Jas a manila envelope, still sealed, and Jas signed for it. With shaky hands she opened it, peered inside and was relieved to see that the ring was still there.

Jas was exhausted from all of the worry, anxiety and excitement. She hadn't been home in five months and was painfully homesick. She wanted to be in familiar surroundings. Luckily, she had a small savings account to which, upon being incarcerated, she had given Yvonne a power of attorney. It was through Yvonne that Jas was able to keep her utilities and payments current.

Although she was exonerated, Jas was concerned that her infamy would keep potential customers from engaging her services as an interior designer. While still in jail, she was contacted by a free-lance writer who asked if she would let him do a story on her. She told him she would think about it and contact him later, but she never did. After all she had been through, she decided she would write her own book and tell the story in her own words. She had been a journalism major in college and the prospect of writing an autobiography excited her. She could publish it as fiction and embellish it a bit. Looking on the bright side, if her business waned, she would have plenty of time to write.

Winston Carlson was taken into custody but he was not booked immediately. Law enforcement wanted to interrogate him before charges were filed. Consequently, Winston spent the night in jail. The next morning he was led into a brightly lit interrogation room where he sat and waited for what seemed like an eternity. The steel table had eyelets riveted to the top for handcuffing hostile detainees. The drab light green paint on the walls was peeling. The floor was dirty and the room smelled like stale liquor. Winston felt nauseous. The emotional trauma of having confessed to a crime he didn't commit and his present surroundings made his stomach churn. He hoped he wouldn't vomit; that would show weakness and that was something he could and would not tolerate. Winston was sick with anticipation not knowing what was happening with Adell. Had they released her as a result of his confession? Was she sitting in a room just like this one? Did she know he confessed? Damn it! Why wouldn't anyone tell him anything?

Two detectives finally came in. They were chatting about the outcome of Jas' trial in general and the previous day's events in particular.

211

Winston asked them what all the excitement was about. They looked at Winston, somewhat irritated, and replied that it was not an everyday occurrence that murder charges against a defendant were dismissed in the middle of trial based on the confession of the purported perpetrator. They explained to Winston that they were directed by their commander to interview him regarding his having admitted to committing the murder.

Winston said caustically, "I'm not making any statement until you tell me what has become of my wife, Adell Carlson."

The detectives looked at each other in amazement. "You mean the woman they arrested for contempt of court for refusing to answer a question?"

"What? What are you saying? You mean she wasn't charged with the murder; that she was taken into custody only for contempt of court for not having answered a question?"

"Of course. Did you think she also confessed to the murder? Man, it's either feast or famine around here. Naw, she refused to answer a question while on the witness stand and the judge ordered her to be jailed.

He did not say for how long. All we know is that there is a hold on her."

"Oh, my God!" Winston exclaimed. "Oh, my God!"

"Now what?"

"I want to recant my confession."

"You're kidding, of course, aren't you?"

"NO! I did not kill McGregor. I'm now denying any involvement."

"Geeze Louise. Get the boss."

Detective Lance Young left the room and Detective Larry Bridges began rummaging his pockets for antacid tablets. Within a matter of minutes Detective Young returned with a stern looking man that Winston assumed was "the boss."

"Hi, Winston. I'm Captain Logan. We've not yet met. I understand you would like to withdraw your confession and are now saying you didn't murder Mr. McGregor. Is that correct?"

"Damn right. I didn't kill the bastard. How do I right the record?"

"Do you want a lawyer?"

"Only if I need one. What would the process be to prove that I didn't do it?"

"A lie detector test would be a good first step."

"All right then, let's do it."

"It's not that easy. We have to set it up and get a technician. We only have two officers who are trained and experienced polygraphists; one is on sick leave having broken his leg skiing up at Purgatory last week. The other has been working his normal duty rotation on the swing shift and he will not be available until shift change this afternoon at 1500. I'll ask you again; do you want to call a lawyer?"

"Yes, since I have to spend most of the day in jail, I have no choice but to call a lawyer."

The telephone was passed to Winston and all three law enforcement officers left the room.

Winston then called the attorney the Carlsons had on retainer for their business. They often needed legal advice during real estate transactions. His name was Andrew Sinclair.

"Andy!" Winston yelled into the phone. "I'm in the slammer and need your help pronto."

"Winston," Sinclair replied, "I'm not a criminal lawyer. My expertise, as you know, is civil. I don't know how much help I would be to you."

"Damn the torpedoes, Andy. Get your ass over here as soon as you can or I'm going to replace you as our attorney."

"Calm down, Winston. I'll be there, I'm just saying…"

"Never mind what you're just saying – just be here. Bring the checkbook. You need to bail both Adell and me out of this place." And with that Winston slammed down the receiver.

Winston spent a fitful morning and afternoon in jail. His cell was cold and the cot was miserably hard. He restlessly paced his cell waiting for something to happen. The minutes were dragging and the only thing to happen was lunch. Winston was much too distraught to eat so he pushed the tray aside and began pacing again. After another eternity passed, Sinclair was admitted into Winston's cell.

"It's about damn time!"

"Winston, I arrived at noon, I've been waiting for over an hour. They refused to let me in until after lunch was cleared. I was advised by the jailer that you requested a polygraph. Have they given you an indication when that would take place?"

"No, they've given me nothing. Can you find out anything, especially what has become of Adell."

"Yes, I did inquire about Adell. Judge Ralston will have to decide what to do with her."

"Why didn't you tell me that sooner?"

"For God's sake, man, I just got here."

"Okay, I know, I'm sorry, I'm so distressed that I don't know what I'm doing or saying. What happens when I pass the polygraph? Will they let me go?"

"I can't say at this point. It all depends on what other evidence they have against you. Do you know of anything other than your confession?"

"No. I was never in that house. They couldn't have much."

"Whatever made you confess in the first place? The jailer told me all about your predicament. Adell's as well. It sounds like the only nail in the coffin is yours."

"I thought Adell was going to be charged with the murder. Anyway that's the way it appeared to me.

When they took her away yesterday in cuffs I thought for sure she was being arrested for Nick McGregor's murder. In order to save her, I decided to confess. "

"Did you explain this to the detectives?"

"No. When I requested an attorney, they quit asking me questions."

"Okay, I'm going to leave now and find out what's going on. You try to calm down. If you're emotionally upset it may have a bearing on the poly. I'll be back as soon as I know something. Okay?"

"Okay. Thanks. I'm sorry I barked at you."

Sinclair left the cell and went to the main desk and asked to speak to the officer in charge. Sergeant Preston, yes, really, Sergeant Preston. Preston came to the front counter where he asked Sinclair what he could do for him.

Suppressing the urge to ask Preston how Yukon King was doing, Sinclair decided the lad was far too young to know anything about the glorious days of yesteryear when radio ruled and Canadian Mounty Police Sergeant Preston and his faithful dog, Yukon King, maintained peace in the Alaskan territory by outsmarting the criminal element who preyed on the

217

innocent. Instead he stated: "I'm representing Winston Carlson and I understand he is scheduled for a polygraph presumably today. Can you tell me at what time that has been scheduled?"

"Looks like, hummm, just about now," Preston said examining his clipboard. "Do you want to be present for the examination?"

"Of course. Where will it be conducted?"

"We have our own facility right here in the detention center. Look, they're bringing your client in now. I'll grease the skids for you so you won't have any problem watching from a connecting room that has a two-way mirror."

Sinclair was granted permission to confer with Winston before the polygraph commenced. After Winston was advised of the protocol, he was ushered into the polygraph room where the police polygrapher administered the test which took less than thirty minutes. While they awaited the test results, Sinclair was asked to remain in a waiting room and Winston was returned to his cell. After approximately forty-five minutes, Sinclair was advised of the results.

Detectives Bridges and Young arrived back at the station house early enough to be present when the results of Winston's polygraph examination were posted.

"I knew it! Damn the luck, I just knew it!" Bridges raved and waved his arms wildly around in frustration. He stormed into his office and called Cooper to pass on the results of the polygraph hoping it wasn't too late for something to be salvaged out of the whole sorry mess. She was not yet in the office having to make the drive from Farmington to Albuquerque after the case against Jas was dismissed. Bridges left word for her to call him IMMEDIATELY upon her return. Cooper didn't carry a cell phone. She would often forget to turn it off in court and was admonished on more than one occasion by the presiding judge so she opted to not carry one at all. It was too humiliating to be dressed down in front of God and everyone else.

Time crawled by as Bridges paced up and down waiting for the call. He continually checked his watch. He telephoned twice more just to make sure Cooper received his message. Finally he got the return call.

"What's up?" Cooper asked.

"Carlson recanted his confession when he learned his wife was only being held on contempt charges. He asked for and took a poly. The sorry sucker thought she was being arrested for the murder and he was playing the martyr in order to save her. He passed the poly and we, of course other than his now withdrawn confession, do not have a shred of evidence to link him to the murder. The local DA's office authorized his release since there is nothing to hold him on. Where do we go from here?"

"Where can we go from here? The case has been dismissed, and with prejudice I might add. We have no recourse. I hate like hell for her to get away with it but…"

"Me too. I'm numb. I'm going home and drain a gallon of gin and sleep for a week. Thanks for the valiant effort. Take it easy, counselor." Bridges replaced the phone in its cradle and headed out the door for home. As she hung up the phone, Cooper was wondering if maybe she could also use a drink or two.

CHAPTER 15

HURRICANE WARNINGS

"Congratulations!" said Sinclair as he was being let back into Winston's cell. "You passed with flying colors and, just as you surmised, the DA has no evidence that you were in or upon the McGregor premises at any time whatsoever. The lab compared your prints and DNA that you provided upon your admittance with samples collected from the crime scene and nothing matched back to you. After I explained why you confessed, the DA decided not to pursue charges against you. They could have nailed you with False Reporting but in light of what a cluster this whole ordeal has turned into they opted not to take any further action. Similarly, Judge Ralston took pity and sentenced Adell to time served and she is also free to go."

"That is wonderful news. Hummm, so, the murder of Nick McGregor still remains a mystery?"

"So it appears. Not our worry. Let's get you processed and out of here."

"Damn straight! I'm ready. Where is Adell now?"

"She is being processed as we speak and we will meet her in the front lobby."

The Carlsons engaged in a long tearful embrace upon seeing each other for the first time since the events of the previous day. "Oh, my Darling, you were willing to sacrifice yourself to save me. I should be angry with you for thinking I did it, but I'm not. I just want you to know that Nick and I were never romantically involved. We were just platonic friends. That's all. I was helping him study for his realtor license. I didn't mention it in court when they started badgering me because even to me it sounded like a lame excuse and besides Nick asked me to keep it a secret. He didn't want it known that he was having financial difficulties and was forced to do something to generate income. He said he started a remodel which turned out to be more expensive than he ever dreamed it would be. In addition, one of his daughters had to have surgery. Her husband was a victim of the failed economy and was out of work and they were not insured. Nick paid the doctor and hospital somewhere in the neighborhood of \$95,000. I promised I would not say anything about him obtaining a realty license and his financial woes. I felt I had to honor that promise, and especially now that he's deceased. I had no idea I could really be put in jail for refusing to answer a question and then after it went on so long, that stubborn streak in me wouldn't let me answer and this was the result. I want you to believe that I am guilty only of stupidity. I know I've not been a good wife but, if you'll give me a chance, I'll make it up to you for the rest of our lives together. I love you, Winston."

"Adell, I've never loved anyone else and could never go on without you. And, I'll hold you to that promise."

Sinclair, brushing a tear or two from his eyes, signed the release forms and silently exited the building. He thought to himself as he unlocked his car, "Thank God I'm a civil lawyer. This crap has been enough to last me the rest of my career. I feel for the criminal defense lawyers who do this day in and day out. No wonder they're a strange breed!"

Douglas "Doug" Goldman II owned and operated *Goldman's Fine Jewelry* located on the main drag in Farmington. The business had been handed down from his grandfather, who had immigrated to America at the onset of World War II, to his father and now to him. Doug had an only son who he hoped someday would carry on the family tradition. Time would tell as his son had his heart set on being a rock star. Doug and Detective Larry Bridges were high school buddies. They had participated in sports together and had formed a bond that had endured the test of time. They were close friends and met at least once a month for a beer, sports, political commentary and sometimes poker.

Larry spotted Doug sitting at the bar nursing a beer at their favorite watering hole, "Benjie's." Larry crept up behind Doug and slapping him on the back harder than intended said: "Hey, you son-of-a-gun, how's life treating you?" Jumping slightly and sloshing beer onto the bar, Doug responded, "Pretty good until you interrupted my musings and spilled my brewski."

"You big cry baby. Guess I'll just have to buy you another."

"Yeah. Wish I'd known the 'cry baby' card worked so well. I could have used it lo these many years. Damn!"

Larry slid onto the stool next to Doug and ordered two beers, one for him and a replacement for Doug. Sitting there, Larry tossed a handful of peanuts into his mouth and looked up and down the bar to see who all was there. As he picked up the latest edition of the Farmington newspaper sitting on the bar, the headlines caught his attention: *"First Degree Murder Dismissed Against Zachary."* Doug, looking over Larry's shoulder read and commented on the headline.

"Can't you cops ever get it right? Wasn't that the case you were working on?"

"Same one," Larry responded. "It wasn't my idea to drop the charges. Jas danced her way out of that one!"

Doug looked at Larry quizzically upon hearing the name Jas. Larry asked why Doug was looking at him so funny.

"That name rings a bell. That is an unusual name and one not easily forgotten." Doug rubbed his head and frowned. Suddenly the lights went on.

"I just realized," Doug declared, "I engraved a ring for the murdered guy, Nick McGregor. It was a very expensive wide gold band showcasing a two caret near perfect diamond. McGregor told me it had belonged to his mother and it was his mother's twenty-fifth anniversary present from his father. McGregor also told me that he and his hopefully soon-to-be fiancé were celebrating one-year of being together this coming July and he was going to surprise her with the ring and a proposal." After a brief pause, Doug continued, "McGregor said he thought the ring inscription would personalize the ring and thus make it *hers* since it had previously belonged to his mother. The reason I remember is that he had it inscribed '*Jas,* Luv *U 4-Ever, Nick.*' Jas, as I said, is a very uncommon name. In fact, I'd never heard it before. When you called the defendant Jas it triggered my memory of the inscription."

Larry, absorbed this revelation in the middle of taking a swig of his beer. Finally realizing the significance he choked, coughed and spewed beer out of his mouth and nostrils. "Son-of-a-bitch! Son-of-a-bitch! Damn it anyway! Would you repeat that? No, never mind, I heard you the first time. Son-of-a-bitch! You still have a record of the engrave?"

The bartender, shaking his head, appeared for the second time in less than ten minutes to wipe up beer spilled by the pair of men.

"Of course, I keep impeccable records…." Doug finally answered and wondered if Larry was going to beat his own head against the bar as he was in such a frantic state.

"Okay, I need the original receipt. Can you do that for me?"

"Absolutely, but what…."

Doug sat there patiently waiting for the explanation he felt certain would be forthcoming. Instead, Larry fumbled for his cell phone and called headquarters. When he reached his captain he explained the situation and suggested that a search warrant be prepared immediately for Jas' home, her business, her car and any other property in her control. Upon completion of the call, he jumped up and asked Doug if he would take him to his store so he could retrieve the engraving receipt.

"Sure, but…"

"Never mind. I'll explain later."

Larry tossed a twenty dollar bill onto the bar and the two men hastily left. Larry followed Doug to the jewelry store. It took less than five minutes for Doug to find the receipt. He did keep impeccable records. Once Larry had the receipt in hand, he thanked Doug and rushed out leaving a dazed Doug in his wake.

Detective Bridges arrived at police headquarters just as the search warrant was completed. The captain proof read it and nodded his approval. As always, the document was perfect. Support staff did their job. Bridges made three copies of the document and, with Detective Young in tow, set out to find the on-call judge to get the affidavit approved and the warrant issued.

"Damn, Larry, you lucky jerk, this establishes the missing link, the motive for Zachary to have killed McGregor. She declared all along they were not in an intimate relationship. Then out of the blue a ring inscribed with his love and devotion for her falls into your lap. My best guess is, knowing what I know about McGregor, he was diddling the Carlson woman, God knows why. Yuck! Obviously, Zachary found out about it, or at least suspected it. The green-eyed monster then took over and bye-bye Nicky."

"Yeah, that's my take on it as well. Now if we can just find the ring and/or any other evidence proving they were screwing around we may have another shot at it. I'm not sure how 'new found evidence' plays into resurrecting the case in light of that dismissal. That's the DA's bailiwick but we'll do our job and let the chips fall where they may."

229

"Right on, Bro. Ain't that little lady gonna be surprised! Here she thought she had a free pass."

The pair of detectives didn't have to search far for a judge as one of the county court judges, James Hunter, having worked late, was just leaving the courthouse in his polished black Mercedes when they drove by on their way out of the police department/justice center parking lot. Larry screeched to a halt and rapidly backed up. He approached the judge's driver's side, badge in hand in case the judge hadn't recognized him, and requested that his honor grant him an audience. The judge was gracious and said he would. Larry explained the situation and asked Judge Hunter to read the affidavit and sign the search warrant. Illuminated by the dome light in the judge's Mercedes, the affidavit was read and approved and the search warrant was issued. The judge always carried an official state seal in the glove compartment of his vehicle so he was able to apply all the legalities and formalities for the warrant to be properly issued. It amounted to curb-side service, judge ala carte.

"Thank you Your Honor," Larry said as he gathered up all three signed and sealed copies.

"Good luck, Son," Judge Hunter replied as he drove off heading for the sanctity of his home and the delicious dinner he knew would be waiting. Judge Hunter did enjoy his wife's cooking and his ample stature was a testimonial to what a good cook she was.

The two detectives drove back to the stationhouse to recruit some uniforms to assist in the search. It was then 9:00 p.m. and, by the time they were ready to roll, it was already 9:30 p.m. Just as well, she was probably in bed. With the no-knock search warrant, Jas would have no time to take evasive action and that way the the ring would not just mysteriously disappear.

⊙⃝⃟⃠

Jas was abruptly awakened by a cracking noise at the front door as the lock was jimmied by the search team. *Oh my God, now what?* Jas slipped on her robe and padded barefoot to the door and was greeted by what she later described to Salty as "a swarm of blues."

"What is going…."

231

"We have a warrant to search your premises and vehicle, Ms. Zachary, here is your copy. Will you just step aside and stay out of the way so we can conduct our search? Thank you."

A confused Jas stepped aside. She looked at the warrant in utter disbelief and retreated into the dining room area and quietly sat at the table keeping a watchful eye on the invaders while one of them kept a watchful eye on her.

The officers scattered each taking a separate section of the condominium. The search was confined to locating and seizing a special item, an engagement ring with a specific engraving. Larry found his way to the master bedroom and looked around for a jewelry box or armoire. He found both inside the walk-in closet. The armoire had a hidden drawer, which was a joke. Even the greenest amateur could have ferreted it out. Inside all cozy and snug in a dark blue velvet ring roll was the sought-after prize. Larry recognized it immediately from Doug's description. "Well, well, well" he thought as he turned it over in his hand reading the inscription: "*Jas, Luv U 4-Ever, Nick.*" Detective Young was searching other areas of the master suite and Larry beckoned him over with a jerk of his head and pointed to the ring's inscription. Lance gave Larry a knowing smile. He had also found an incriminating piece of evidence, Jas' photo album containing "up close and personal" pictures of the couple taken during their relationship. He showed the album to Larry and they high-fived each other. "How sweet it is!" hissed Larry as he bagged his treasure trove.

After the search was concluded, Larry told Jas to get dressed and she was once again placed in custody and transported to police headquarters. She was isolated in the same interrogation room she had occupied many months before. The only thing she said was "I demand my right to call my attorney." The detectives knowing they could not deny this request handed her the phone and hastily left the room.

"Sam, I've been arrested again. Will you please come, I need your help. I'll explain when you get here."

Salty arrived at the police station in less than an hour. When he asked the officers what Jas was being held for he was informed they had "newly discovered evidence" and would be requesting the DA to re-file the first degree murder prosecution against Jas.

"What? That's ridiculous! The case was dismissed *with prejudice* and jeopardy has attached. Even if she confessed you couldn't bring her to trial again."

"That's the DA's call. We are in the process now of informing Ms. Cooper of what has come to light. A copy of the warrant and inventory is being faxed to Albuquerque."

"May I be so bold as to also be privy to 'what has come to light?'"

Detective Bridges gave Salty a copy of the search warrant including the affidavit therefor and the inventory of items taken into evidence, the fruits of the search so to speak. The first item was, of course, the ring. Salty read and re-read the listed inscription. He shook his head and read it again. He didn't want to believe what he was seeing because he, too, instantly connected the dots. He sat down heavily in one of the visitor's chairs staring out into space completely flabbergasted by this new revelation. After the shock diminished, Salty asked to see his client. He was led into the interrogation room. Jas was seated at the table with her head buried in her folded arms. She looked up when he entered. Her first inclination was to run to him but she quickly discarded that notion when she saw the look of disgust and disappointment on his face. Salty put his finger to his lips silencing her in case she was tempted to blurt out anything. He simply said that he would visit her in jail early the next day. With that he left and Jas was alone wallowing in oceans of reflection and desertion. Sam was stoic and she could only imagine what he must be thinking and feeling. Tomorrow was light years away and way too far out of reach.

Jas had invoked her right to an attorney and the detectives knew it was useless and indeed a violation of the law to attempt to interrogate her. So, they left the jail crew to process her into custody. The same routine was conducted as before. A mug shot was taken, she was fingerprinted, her personal items were confiscated, she was issued an orange jump suit, jailhouse slippers and cheap hygiene items. She was led to a pod to begin the dreadful night in the cold of her lonely cell. Woeful anticipation was interrupted by fitful sleep. Déjà vu.

When Salty was escorted to Jas' cell the following morning, she looked like a train wreck. Salty entered and sat down next to her on the cot. He started to say something but Jas put her hand over his mouth and whispered, "Shhhhh, this time I am Shahrazad. I will tell the story."

"NO! Don't say a word," Salty said with authority. "You don't have to; I don't want to know. Your case has been dismissed with prejudice. You can never be retried for the same crime regardless of circumstances – even so-called newly discovered evidence. You can only be retried if the case had been dismissed *without* prejudice. There is no need for you to explain anything to me or to anyone else. If the DA decides to re-file the case, we will obtain a writ to prohibit prosecution and even take it to the highest court in the land if need be, the United States Supreme Court. The U.S. Constitution, more particularly, the Fifth Amendment, clearly states that no one can be tried twice for the same crime. To bring charges again would result in placing you in *double jeopardy* which, as I say, is a no-no."

"But I. . . Okay, you're my attorney and I will take your advice."

"Smart Lady! Who do those clowns think they are? I'm going to obtain your release as soon as possible. We may have to wait for Cooper to make her decision on recharging. If she is as smart as I give her credit for, she will pass on this one. At any rate, we will be able to bail you out pending any appeal in the event the judge allows a re-filing."

"Sam, I want you to…"

"NO! Do not ever mention it again. Am I clear on that point? Never again!"

Jas was confused as to why Sam was so adamant about not wanting to know the facts but, she had to admit to herself, she was relieved at not having to explain what really happened.

Salty was now so much in love with Jas that he didn't want her confession to come between them. He surmised what must have happened and if he didn't have the details, that was fine. He didn't need them. There was nothing she could reveal that would change his feelings for her – not even complicity. As he prepared to leave, Salty took her hand and squeezed it in a gesture of support and confidence. She squeezed back what Salty interpreted as her trust and, also he hoped, her love.

⊚⊶⊷⊶⊷⊶☾

Bridges spent the better part of an hour on the phone with Cooper outlining the newly discovered evidence, which consisted mainly of the inscription on the ring and the incriminating photo album. Cooper listened with interest and, knowing it was a long shot, decided to move to re-file the case based on the newly discovered evidence. Under the circumstances, that was the only way justice could be served. Her instincts told her it was probably a futile effort but she was still incensed that Zachary had literally gotten away with murder. She knew they had the right person but when Winston Carlson confessed, she was obligated, though impulsively, to proceed the way she did.

"All right, Detective, I'll bring the motion with me to Farmington first thing tomorrow. Will you see if you can get us on the docket and inform defense counsel of the date and time of the hearing? Don't get your hopes up. We're travelling in uncharted waters here and the judge may well invoke the barrier erected by the *double jeopardy* clause of the U.S. Constitution."

"I'll make sure we're on the docket. Thanks, Counselor."

When Salty was informed by Detective Bridges that the prosecution was filing a motion to re-file the case based on newly discovered evidence he didn't know whether to laugh or cry. The hearing was set for 2:30 p.m. the following afternoon which gave him ample time to prepare a response. With the facts and the law on his side, he was confident the defense would prevail. He went by the jail to see Jas and told her what was happening and that he would address bond at the hearing and hopefully get her out of jail that same day in the event the re-filling was authorized. He then returned to his office to prepare the response.

At precisely 2:30 p.m., court was called to order and Judge Ralston took the bench.

"I understand there is a motion in the case of *People of the State of New Mexico v. Jasmine Zachary.* Ms. Cooper…"

"Yes, Your Honor. The People of the State of New Mexico have newly discovered evidence which further implicates Ms. Zachary as the perpetrator of the crime charged and the prosecution is requesting permission to re-file the case in light of this discovery. As Your Honor is aware, Winston Carlson was cleared by law enforcement of having murdered Nick McGregor. His bogus confession, of course, was the basis of the dismissal of the charges previously filed against Ms. Zachary."

Judge Ralston stated, staring into space, "I have a copy of the motion and the defendant's response before me. I have read both. The response carries a lot of weight regarding *double jeopardy*. However, in the interests of justice, I will grant your motion to re-file."

Salty instantly was on his feet. "Judge," Salty began, "may I be heard?"

"Go ahead, Mr. Morton."

"I intend to contest the decision allowing the prosecution leave to re-file charges and I will be filing a petition for a Writ of Prohibition with the Supreme Court. In the interim, I'm requesting that the court allow Ms. Zachary to be released from custody on her own recognizance."

"Mr. Morton, this is a capital case. Do you seriously expect me to grant a PR bond to the defendant? I will, in the alternative, set bond and $200,000."

"Thank you, Your Honor," replied Salty and he wondered why counsel always thanked the judge whether the decision was favorable or adverse as in the present instance. Knowing that he would be held in contempt if he said what he really thought about the judge's decision, he wisely opted to keep mum. Restraint was the better part of valor.

"Ms. Cooper, do you have anything else?"

"No, Your Honor."

"Mr. Morton?"

"Nothing at this time Your Honor," Salty responded solemnly as he sat mentally composing his writ.

Before they parted, Salty looked at Jas and told her he would see about bail. The appellate process could take a while and he didn't want her sitting in jail another six months. Salty had a cousin who was a local bondsman. After leaving the courthouse, he called "Williams Bail Bonds" and talked to Butch Williams, his cousin and sole owner of the company. "Hey, Butch, how goes the battle?"

"Salty, you old dog, where ya been?"

"Busy, my friend, very busy. I have a favor to ask you. Have you been following the Zachary murder case?"

"Hasn't everyone?"

"As you know Jas is my client. The prosecution just filed a motion which was granted to re-file the case on the basis of newly discovered evidence. When the case was dismissed the first time, jeopardy attached and no matter what the circumstances, Jas cannot constitutionally be retried for the same crime. She has been rearrested pending the outcome of the writ I am seeking to obtain from the Supreme Court. The judge has set bond at $200,000. If you would post the $200,000 bond to get her released, I will guarantee that you will not lose it. I would post it myself but I don't have immediate access to that much cash or sureties on such short notice and I don't want to see Jas remain in jail over the weekend. I know you have assets on hand because that's your business. What say you?"

"Salty, old man, since you're a blood relative - and even if you weren't - I trust you when you say you do not intend to lose. So, out of respect, deference, courtesy and friendship, I will do it. I'm also counting on you giving your word that the defendant will not flee the state pending the outcome of the hearing."

"Butch, you have my word and I will make sure that does not happen. If for some unforeseen reason it does, I will personally reimburse you the amount of the bond. Also, I will have my runner deliver a check to you for $20,000.00 representing the 10% bond premium the minute I hang up. Butch, I owe you one. Thanks."

"You owe me nothing, Cous. Take care. I'll get over to the courthouse within the hour and do everything I can to expedite the process."

And so he did. Jas was released from jail on bond later that day and Salty was there to pick her up and be at her side as he had been from the beginning – and not just physically but in mind and heart as well.

As they were preparing to leave the jail, Jas, having retrieved her personal belongings once again put the small gold cross pendant around her neck. While toying with it she said to Salty: "Sam, I have never had the opportunity to pay my last respects to Nick. Would it be too much to ask you to take me by the cemetery so I may say a proper goodbye?"

"Of course I'll take you," Salty replied. "You know he was cremated and is entombed in the mausoleum at Holy Trinity. I visited there right after I took your case so I know exactly where to go. You're sure you want to do this?"

"Yes, I'm sure. I think personally saying goodbye would provide me some closure to this nightmare. With all that has happened, this would ease my conscience.

Paying my respects, plus going to confession and atoning for my many sins is the least I can do! Oh, God, I'm so very sorry I killed him. If only I could undo what I have done and change the course of history.

"Where'd you go?" asked Salty. "I lost you there for a minute."

"I was just thinking about the past two years and how fast one's life can change. I know I haven't told you how very much I appreciate you defending me and having faith and trust in me. 'Appreciate' is not even close to what I feel for you but for lack of a better word..." Tears filled her eyes and Salty took her in his arms and after his tender consolation and tears of his own, Jas continued: "Sam, I would not have made it without you. You kept me going that five months I spent in jail. I looked so forward to your visits. They were all I had to look forward to. When I was ready to just hang it up and just give up, you would appear with your upbeat attitude and buoy me up. It was you who gave me the inspiration, courage and hope to continue." She continued, "Throughout my life I've always thought it was important to tell people in your life how you felt about them: your parents, your husband, your kids, your friends and, of course, your lovers. I've learned that just thinking someone knows or should know, without you actually verbally expressing your feelings, can lead to severe misunderstandings and

245

often result in unintended consequences. I can't even put in words how I feel about you and all you've done for me."

"Hey," Salty replied while still holding Jas in his arms, "you're my client. That's the least I could do. Besides, you deserved it." Salty was hesitant to bear his own soul at this time knowing that Jas was referring to Nick, her past relationship with Nick and the guilt she felt for having killed Nick all because of a lack of understanding and poor communications.

When they arrived at the cemetery, Salty gave Jas directions to the mausoleum and told her he would wait for her in the car. Jas, on shaky legs, made her way to the site. When she saw Nick's name on the brass plate attached to the cement square that sealed his ashes inside the small compartment she began to weep. Then grief stricken, she fell to her knees. Her body racked with sobs. "Oh, Nick, I'm so sorry. Oh, my darling, I'm so, so sorry. I miss you so much and always will." After remaining in this position for a long time, she eventually regained her composure. What was done, was done. She would give anything to take it all back but life goes on. She stood up, wiped her eyes, straightened her clothing and turned to leave. As she approached the wrought iron gate adorned with two winged angles standing guard over the cemetery, she turned and, looking back at the place where Nick's remains rested, threw him her signature departing kiss for the last time. "Goodbye, my darling; rest in peace. I will love you forever."

∘⊶⊰⊱⊷∘

On the ride home, Salty suggested they stop for lunch. He hadn't eaten since the previous day and thought she probably hadn't eaten much either. She flashed him a quick shy smile and readily accepted. She wasn't looking forward to facing the mess created by the search of her home. They stopped at a restaurant that was still serving breakfast. Bacon, eggs, pancakes and hot coffee sounded like heaven – and so it was. They both ate heartedly and kept the conversation light during the meal. Salty occasionally would catch Jas looking quizzically at him while they ate. She finally couldn't stand the suspense and just out-and-out asked him why he didn't want to know what really had happened. She sat toying with the small gold cross pendant waiting for Salty's response. Salty had been mentally reviewing Jas' previous declaration that it was important to tell people how you felt about them and not leave it to chance. After a long pause, a very long pause, which made Jas uncomfortable not knowing what was coming but dreading it anyway, Salty simply said: "I want to get to know you outside the realm of attorney/client. I want to take you places and experience a life with you in which I've never let myself indulge. In case you didn't know, I've fallen in love with you and my fondest hope is that you could love me, too." He looked into those innocent big blue eyes searching for a glimmer of encouragement. Suddenly, she surprised him by throwing her arms around his neck and kissing him full on the lips.

"Oh, Sam! Let's give ourselves a chance to be happy together. I would very much like that. Please be patient and give me time to heal. I'm trying to fight my attraction to you but it's not working. You're too irresistible."

Salty's heart soared with the thought that she could open herself up and give their relationship a chance to grow into love. After lunch he dropped her off at her condo and returned to the office to prepare his writ of prohibition and memorandum of authority, which turned out to be a piece of cake considering he had the facts, the undisputed law and the United States Constitution on his side.

Salty was so encouraged and excited about dating Jas that he could hardly wait to invite her out. He had dated in the past but only casually and no one had ever affected him the way Jas did. The next day he called and asked her to dinner that evening. Jas, having been incarcerated for so long, was more than eager to have some fun so she readily accepted his invitation. She had lost so much weight while incarcerated that her clothes no longer fit nor, for that matter, suited the occasion. Desiring to look her best, she spent the afternoon shopping for a few things.

Salty was punctual and Jas was ready when he arrived. Salty thought she looked stunning in her black slacks and white silk blouse. He was taken aback by her natural beauty which was accented by her stylish hairdo and cameo facial features. Her inviting smile and ingratiating manner was something Salty had not noticed before. Normally, not at a loss for words, Salty managed to say, "I like the transition. You could not look lovelier!"

Jas blushed and said, "That's a nice thing to say. And, you Sir look most handsome."

Salty was not ordinarily bashful but to hear this kind of compliment, especially from this beautiful creature, was unnerving to say the least. He felt an excitement he thought was reserved only for the young.

There was an awkward moment when neither uttered a word. But then again they didn't need to. Their eyes said it all!

"Well, Prince Charming," Jas finally said, "where are you carrying me off to?"

"Not where I'd like to. But then again maybe that's something to look forward to."

Jas was not quite sure if she heard Sam right and didn't have a clever quip. So, she just smiled and filed his comment away for the moment – at least for the *proper* moment.

"I'm sorry," Salty said, "I assume you are asking where I'm taking you for dinner."

"It's your call.   Never do your decisions disappoint."

"I hear they have great prime rib at The River Side. Does that sound good to you?"

Jas froze. That was where she and Nick had their first date and where Nick's daughters had the surprise birthday party. Dining there would only revive memories, some of which she didn't care to revisit. She needed a fresh start. The past with Nick was the past; her future with Sam started now.

"Know what, Sam? I've been craving Mexican cuisine. I think I'd really like to go to Francisco's."

"Ah ha, you do have good taste. That really hits the spot with me. Francisco's is my all-time favorite restaurant. So, Francisco's it is!"

Salty extended his arm and escorted her to his vehicle. Jas was somewhat subdued on the ride to the restaurant but once they ordered and the margaritas arrived she became more relaxed and conversant. Salty understood only too well her fear and trepidation and, not wanting to crowd her, gave her the space she needed and deserved. The two did not escape the attention of the other diners, many of whom they both

251

knew. A few stopped and engaged in casual chatter. However, for the most part Salty and Jas were given the cold shoulder and were the subject of idle gossip. This did not deter either Salty or Jas. Neither minded that they were objects of dinner conversation. Both were ready for whatever the future held in store for them. If they were scorned, then so be it!

Salty, having never married and having lived a simple life had amassed a substantial fortune. That was common knowledge. He had enough for the two to live on comfortably, even extravagantly, for the rest of their lives. He wasn't worried about the adverse consequences that might be generated because of his involvement with a former client, especially one charged with first degree murder. After all, the charges were ultimately dismissed. Regardless, he didn't care at this stage in his career what people thought.

Salty reached across the table and squeezed Jas' hand in a gesture of affection and commitment. Jas squeezed back a reciprocal gesture and smiled longingly at him. Jas looked radiant in the candle light magnifying the newfound happiness within. Both savored an evening of excited anticipation. Their first date heralded in a new season of unprecedented romance for both.

◎◈◈◈◎

As soon as she could after her release from jail, Jas had driven to Aztec to make a confession as required by her faith. She wanted to go to an obscure church where she wouldn't be recognized. Anonymity to her was crucial. Although the Catholic Church had started using face-to-face confessionals several years before, one could still remain incognito by kneeling behind the screen that separated the priest from the penitent rather than the face-to-face concept. There was little likelihood that she would be recognized in Aztec. She was basically driven to make this confession. She thought if she died with so many mortal sins on her soul she would surely spend eternity in hell.

Before embarking on her quest, she researched the Catholic dictates concerning the Seal of Confession and learned that priests could not disclose anything they heard from penitents during the course of the Sacrament of Penance. To do so would result in excommunication of the priest. Jas breathed a sigh of relief learning that

253

she could confess and not be subject to legal recrimination. Even though "jeopardy had attached" she still was not secure in the belief that she was totally free since she had already been arrested twice for the same crime and was possibly facing a second prosecution.

Jas found the church easily enough as she had been there with Yvonne once or twice in the past. San Jose Catholic Church, a Spanish-style church, had been dedicated over a century before. It had an exterior of beige stucco and seven steps leading to the massive double front doors fashioned of oak with brass hardware. There was a steeple on the roof which housed an old bell that had come from a church that had been burned in Aqua Prieta Sonora Mexico. The bell was transported by the faithful to New Mexico to remind them of their Mexican roots and especially their ancestors who had died in the fire.

The fire was suspicious and thought to have been set on purpose by rebels protesting the Holy See's stand on various issues. The doors to the old church had been bolted from the outside preventing the parishioners from escaping. Approximately one hundred and fifty men, women and children died a horrific death standing up for their faith. The source of the fire was never determined. The remainder of the small community lived in fear for their own lives. They packed up their belongings along with the charred bell from the burned church, and made their way to New Mexico. They settled in the small community of Aztec.

Eventually they built another San Jose, a church named after the church in Aqua Prieta that had burned. The masonry and carpentry were intricate and masterful considering the meager tools with which the small band had to work. The pews were hand-carved and the altar was honed from the natural stone found in the surrounding terrain.

The statues of Mary, Joseph and Baby Jesus were created by the women in much the same fashion as they created pottery. One of the survivors was an artist who painted the statues so expertly that they appeared life-like. They were captivating and revered. The crucifix was carved from roughhewn oak and the crucified Jesus was created and painted in the same fashion as the other icons. Miraculously, the paint had

255

not faded or chipped over time. Those visitors who came to view them believed the statues had been protected by God.

The interior of the church was cool and dim. The only light came from the stained glass windows, the rack of votive candles that were lit by loved ones to gain indulgences for the faithfully departed, and the eternal lamps that burned to the right of the altar at the foot of a statue of Mary, the blessed Mother of Christ. The crucifix was suspended above the altar depicting a suffering Christ dying on the cross.

Upon entering the church, Jas genuflected and made the sign of the cross. She observed a line of penitents waiting their turn in the confessional. She joined the line. As she waited, she mentally recounted all the sins to which she would have to confess and winced at the thought of all the evil she had committed. She was truly sorry for having offended her Lord and prayed for the strength to get through her confession without forgetting anything.

Soon it was her turn. Her stomach churned and she wondered if she was going to be sick. Steeling herself against the urge to flee, she entered the confessional. The priest was cordial and invited her to begin her confession. Fearing she would lose her resolve, she blurted out everything she mentally rehearsed hardly stopping to take a breath and then dissolved into tears.

The stunned young priest was speechless. This was the first time anyone had confessed to him of having committed a murder. He didn't know how to proceed so he asked her for details. She said she would rather not expound on the circumstances. She stated she was there to get absolved of her sins for which she was truly sorry and repentant. The priest was silent for a long period as he sat reflecting and praying for guidance. He ultimately concluded that, according to scripture, on the road to Damascus, Jesus interacted with Saul, forgave him for killing Christians, changed Saul's name to Paul and commissioned him to spread the good news. How could he, a humble priest and servant of God, do less than Jesus?

Waiting, Jas fidgeted. She thought he was probably debating whether to forgive her or not. *There I go again trying to read others' thoughts and feelings. That's how I got into this mess in the first place.* The priest finally said he would absolve her of her sins but her penance would be great. He didn't know if this was protocol or not but sensed it was divine intervention so he told Jas she would have to make recompense to the victim's family in some fashion and say a rosary every day for a year for the soul of her victim. Relieved she was forgiven, she would have agreed to any penance. She was actually surprised that the penance wasn't more considering the gravity of her sins.

After making a perfect Act of Contrition, Jas thanked the priest and left the confessional. She then slid into a pew in the rear of the church. Making the familiar sign of the cross she silently prayed: "Thank you God for giving me the strength to follow through with my confession. I feel like the weight of the world has been lifted from my shoulders. I know I will still have to atone for my many transgressions in Purgatory but you know my heart and that I am truly sorry for having sinned against you. I include Nick in my Act of Contrition. Please forgive him. He didn't have a chance to repent. I robbed him of that. Not only did I kill him but I stole paradise from him as well. Loving, merciful and gracious Father, I beseech you to make allowances for Nick. I promise that I will live the rest of my life making up for the severe damage I've caused. Please send me a sign that Nick is forgiven, I will not rest until I know. I ask this in Jesus' name. Amen."

Jas slowly stood and made her way to the exit. She crossed herself with holy water and looking back towards the confessional, issued a sigh of relief. She then turned and moved out into the sunlight. As she stood on the steps adjusting to the brightness of the day, a group of school children filed past under the watchful eye of an elderly nun. Jas watched as they passed. Still watching, Jas saw one of the young boys turn and, as though the miracle she had asked for was manifesting itself before her very eyes, the child threw her a kiss mirroring the traditional departure kiss she ceremoniously threw to Nick throughout their relationship. She also noticed the boy's smile. It was a smile etched in her memory – Nick's smile. A stunned Jas turned back to the church, folded her hands together in prayer and said out loud, "Thank you, God. Thank you. Thank you. Thank you." Jas had turned toward the church only momentarily. When she looked back to where she had observed the young boy, she could scarcely believe her eyes – not by what she saw, but by what she didn't see. There was no sign of the boy or anyone else. All had disappeared as quickly as they had appeared.

On the drive home, still in disbelief pondering the mystery of what had just occurred, Jas wondered what she could do for recompense to Nicole and Nick's other daughters. It was important to her to satisfy her penance as soon as possible; especially in light of having experienced what she believed was a miracle. Suddenly she had an epiphany. She would sell the ring and split the proceeds between the four girls. She had little else of value. Her savings had been depleted during the five months she was incarcerated and she still didn't know what Sam was going to charge for her defense. After all, Nick had bought the ring (or so she surmised) so, in essence, it should be part of his daughters' inheritance. Jas speculated a wide gold band with a large diamond should be worth quite a bit. She also recognized that parting with it would be extremely painful as she thought of it as proof of Nick's love for her. Then again, perhaps pain was part of the reconciliation process. She didn't need anything tangible by which to remember Nick. His memory would forever be etched in her heart, mind and soul. So, the decision was easy. She would sell the ring as soon as possible and anonymously distribute the proceeds to Nick's daughters.

Salty read and reread his petition for a writ of prohibition and at the end of the day decided the document was all-inclusive and met all the legal requirements. The basic fundamental right of all American citizens was the right not to be tried twice for the same crime thus not to be placed in *double jeopardy*. Salty was more than pleased with his creation. He mailed the original of the document accompanied by ten copies to the New Mexico Supreme Court. He filed a copy with the San Juan County District Court and mailed another copy to Cooper.

Cooper's response and brief in opposition to Salty's petition was filed well in advance of the deadline. That in itself was miraculous as filing anything early was unheard of. Attorneys were notorious for pressing up against deadlines and pressuring themselves and their staff into ulcers and heart attacks. Her response rested on equitable grounds since there was not much else to rely on. It read: *The ends of justice, in light of the newly discovered incriminatory evidence, cries out for prosecution. The greatest good for the greatest number should trump a guilty individual's claim of double jeopardy. No one is above the law and no one should profit from his or her own misdeeds.*

Salty was confident his double jeopardy argument would stand up especially at the State Supreme Court level. Still there was that lingering doubt. Thus began the long agonizing wait.

After the first week, Salty checked the mail daily hoping for a decision which he knew would not be rendered for some weeks. The court's docket was always back-logged but Salty was anxious. Jas' freedom was hanging in the balance. At the end of the fifth week alas the decision was finally rendered. Salty carelessly tore open the envelope and hastily thumbed to the last page.   There he read the high court's opinion:

THE COURT FINDS in accordance with the Constitution of New Mexico and the Constitution of the United States as follows: The case of *People of the State of New Mexico, Plaintiff v. Jasmine Zachary, Defendant,* cannot be re-filed nor the aforesaid Defendant retried. This Court upholds the Defendant's position as outlined in her petition for Writ of Prohibition. Our ruling is that jeopardy attached upon dismissal with prejudice at the first trial and to re-file the case or retry the Defendant would result in double jeopardy which is clearly in violation of the Constitution of the State of New Mexico as well as the Constitution of the United States.

IT IS THE COURT'S ORDER, therefore, that the Defendant, Jasmine Zachary, be and is hereby exonerated and declared immune from criminal prosecution on the pending charges.   The case, therefore, is dismissed with prejudice for all time never again to be resurrected.

DONE BY THE COURT:
 /s/ Corbin J. Dominguez___
Chief Justice of the
New Mexico Supreme Court

EPILOGUE

"Okay, people, that's a wrap." Bishop shouted to the *Sincerely Yours* crew. Her team members jumped into action, yanking on cords and disassembling lights and camera stands. Bishop nodded approvingly and smiled at Salty, extending her hand. He rose from behind the desk.

"Thank you, Salty, for the interview. What a fascinating story. It will be a few weeks before we actually air the segment, but I will let you know the exact date and time so you can watch."

She stuffed a sheaf of papers into her bag and turned to go. She hesitated for a moment and then turned back to look at Salty. "OK, you've got to tell me. Don't leave me hanging on this one. Whatever happened to your client?"

At that exact moment, the door to the outside office swung open and a stunning auburn haired beauty entered. Bishop watched as Salty rounded his desk and went to greet the visitor. He lightly kissed the woman's cheek then proffered his arm. She gently looped her arm through his as he escorted her back to his office where the crew was removing the last pieces of equipment.

"Ms. Bishop, I'd like to introduce my wife, Jasmine Morton.   Jas, this is Linda Bishop, a reporter from *Sincerely Yours*.   We just finished an interview featuring my most interesting career case."   He hesitated for a moment and smiled.   "Can you guess which one I chose?"   Jas smiled at a stunned Linda Bishop as the two shook hands.   She then looked up at Salty, and toying with the small gold cross pendant hanging around her neck, coyly responded, "No, darling. Please tell me, which one did you choose?"
"The one with the happy ending," Salty replied, gazing into Jas' innocent big blue eyes, "the one with the happy ending."

… and so it ends…

ABOUT THE AUTHOR

Judith Blevins has spent her entire professional life experiencing the mystery, intrigue and courtroom drama that unfolds daily within the criminal justice system. Her previous experience as a court clerk, then serving five consecutive district attorneys in Grand Junction, Colorado, has provided the inspiration for her first novel, *Double Jeopardy.*

Ms. Blevins is also working on a soon to be released series of children's books written in collaboration with fellow author, Carroll Multz.